Focus

By: Naomi Charles

Focus

First paperback edition August 2020
Second paperback edition August 2023

Cover art and design by OkayCreations

ISBN 978-1-7352292-8-7

Chapter 1

Whoever created the concept of surprises was a sick human being. Surprises are like the jump scares you see in horror movies, but instead of screaming, you have to laugh and act like it's completely fine, except it's not. If you're not picking up what I'm putting down, I don't do surprises. Risks and danger were not my thing. Never have been and never will. The idea of willingly putting oneself in a situation where they won't know the outcome until it happens put a sour taste in my mouth. I hated not knowing what was going to happen, so you can imagine the horror I felt when the letter that would determine whether I would be going to my dream school came in the mail.

You would've thought the contents of the envelope sitting on our coffee table were the answer to whether I would live to see tomorrow. There was fear in each and every one of our eyes. Dad jumped when Mom reached forward and grabbed the envelope. She inspected it as if something on it could've changed with us all sitting there, looking at it.

She glanced at me before looking at the fold where it was glued shut. *Oh no.* She was about to open it, and I wasn't ready.

"We should just burn it honestly… There's no need to even look at it," I said.

Mom and Dad looked up at the sound of my voice. It had been quiet for so long that it was almost startling to hear something besides the sound of the fire crackling in the marble fireplace. Mom finally cracked a smile and started laughing.

"Nicole, don't be ridiculous. Just open it," she said as she held the envelope out for me.

I grabbed the envelope but couldn't open it. Instead, I stared at it up close. All eyes were on me by then.

"I just don't take rejection well." I sighed.

"Rejection doesn't always mean things won't work out… Your mother told me no four times before she went on a date with me," Dad chimed in.

"That's lovely… I don't think it works like that, though," I deadpanned.

"Just open it already!" Mom almost screamed.

I rolled my eyes and sat up straight in my chair. I said a little prayer in my head as I tore it open. I looked up at my parents, and they were staring at me as they held hands tightly. They were nervous too. I pulled the letter out of the envelope and read the first word–congratulations. I screamed and stood up.

"Baby, who needs NYU." Dad shrugged, trying to play it cool, even though I could see the sadness in his eyes.

"No! No… I… I'm in! I got accepted! Oh my God!" I jumped so high that I was surprised I didn't hit the chandelier hanging from the ceiling.

"Like I said, NYU only accepts the best," he said, and Mom laughed at his error.

"That's my girl, Dr. Nicole Smith," Mom said, letting go of Dad and pulling me in for a hug.

Dad soon joined us, and I was almost smothered by all the love. I was so happy that tears started to run down my cheeks. Things were turning out to be ok.

I woke up to a low tapping sound. My eyes opened to almost no light at all. It was still night. I checked my phone, and it was one in the morning. I heard the tapping sound again, faint with the white noise of the air system to combat the summer heat. I looked around my room, everything seemed to be in place. The tapping sound happened again, only a little louder. That was when I saw a shadow by my window. I pulled my bat from under my bed and slowly walked toward it. The worst things came to mind. I pulled the curtains to the side and tightened my grip on the bat. After a few deep breaths, I leaned in to see who it was. My heart was beating like I had just run a mile. My eyes focused on the figure and caught a glimpse of the sparkling of sequins that reflected into my room. I realized it was just Rachel, my sister. I dropped the bat and opened my window up for her.

"You over everyone should know to not do that to me. What happened to a phone call?" I asked as I turned the light on.

"Sorry… You weren't answering your phone. Are you going to do the *bat thing* when you move out?" Rachel asked in a hushed tone when she climbed in.

"Yeah, especially if someone taps on my window on the third floor… Also, some of us have normal sleeping schedules." I sighed as I handed her a T-shirt and shorts so she wouldn't be caught by Mom and Dad in her party outfit.

"Who would it have been besides me?" she scoffed.

She had her curls out. It framed her round face like a mane. Her gold earrings chimed whenever she moved. They went perfectly with her milk chocolate skin. She always wore a smile that made you want to nestle up and get warm by the fire that was inside her. It was so easy to share your secrets with Rachel, but this time I ignored her question. I wasn't in the mood to talk about *that*.

"What am I going to do without you when you're in the city unable to come to my rescue," she said, throwing her party clothes on the floor and changing into the clothes I handed her.

"Is that what you want me around for? Only to help you with your late-night escapades?" I rolled my eyes.

"Not the only thing… I'm going to miss you, Coco. You better come home and visit often," she said, climbing in bed next to me.

"Girl, there is not enough room for you in this bed," I said, sliding over.

"You leave in a couple days. Let me live." She laughed, and I did too.

The days leading up to me moving to the city involved friends and family coming over to help me pack before I left. It was really nice, but it also really wasn't. I preferred being alone. *Nicole, college won't be like high school. Nicole, you'll have to be responsible since Mom and Dad won't be around.* I knew things were going to be different. I didn't need everyone to remind me of it.

"I'm going to miss you so much. Watch us never get the chance to coordinate coming home at the same time because you're out there being involved in ten thousand things," Michelle said as she packed my clothes into a bin.

Michelle and I had been friends since middle school. She was my best friend. I thanked God every day for allowing her to put up with me. I knew I wasn't always the easiest to deal with. Michelle always helped me put things in perspective or just reminded me to use logic in general when I had my moments. Those moments used to happen often. They still happened, but thankfully, far less. Michelle was a middle-aged mom in an eighteen-year old's body. She was athletic from her years of cheerleading with me and had the most perfect dark chocolate skin. She looked like she would be this fun model type. Nevertheless, underneath all that, she was just a mom. She always knew what to say and what to do when things went wrong. I envied her calmness. I didn't have a calm bone in my body.

What was the point of college when you already have a degree in overthinking with a minor in worrying?

"That's old-Nicole. New-and-wiser-Nicole takes things easy," I said, not even convinced myself, but *fake it until you make it*, they say.

The plan for my first semester was to take things easy. I wouldn't get overly involved in school like I used to. I wouldn't take extra classes when I didn't need to. I would simply get acclimated to the city and school life. Maybe I would even hang out occasionally—just nothing dangerous or risky. The way I saw it, there would be way less issues that way.

"You started taking things easy because of... you know... the breakup. Things will be different in college. You might even find a guy," Michelle said, hesitantly. She was always careful with bringing that topic up.

"Right... because of the breakup... Anyway, I'm not looking for anyone this semester. It's time to focus on school and my future career," I said, quickly changing the topic.

"Oh my God... speaking of relationships... look who it is," she said, holding up a picture frame.

I hesitated to walk over, but I finally did. It was exactly what I expected, a picture of Noah Crawford and I in each other's arms. *Of course*, we look super happy in it. Recently, thinking about him hurt a lot less and made me feel a lot less crazy about missing him sometimes. Even though it threw me off a lot less, its effect on me was still felt. It was not something I was proud of, and no, I never spoke to anyone about it. I couldn't. It was complicated. Whenever I thought about Noah, I thought about what happened and more importantly the last day I ever saw him.

***

I crawled up into a ball and started crying uncontrollably. No, it wasn't the type of crying that you say is uncontrollable but really is controllable. This was involuntary. I tried to stop, but it was as if I never tried. I finally looked up and Noah was looking back at me with tears running down his face. Even after everything, seeing him cry broke my heart. I wanted to reach out and wipe the tears from his eyes, but I couldn't stop shaking.

"How could you do this? I can't believe you made me do all of that… All of that… just for you to leave," I croaked.

"I know… I'm so sorry." He gave a painful sigh.

***

Michelle sneezed from the dust of all the moved furniture in my room, and it pulled me out of my thoughts. I grabbed the frame and faced it down on my shelf. I was done looking at Noah's face.

"Don't you think it's time to move on? It's been two years, Nicole." Michelle frowned.

"Don't you think we should not waste our time talking about some dumb guy?" I crossed my arms over my chest to show bravado, but also to stop my heart from racing.

"Fine, but all I'm saying is… be open. You can't hold onto what happened forever," Michelle said knowingly.

I nodded. *Oh Michelle, if only you knew*, I thought.

Chapter 2

Ever since I received my acceptance letter from NYU earlier in the year, Mom and Dad had gotten an obscene amount of apparel with those three letters on it. I was pretty sure they had gotten more college apparel than I did, and yes, I was excited. I just did not have the desire to be a walking billboard every day. When people would ask if they had gone to NYU, they would say no but their daughter was. They were very proud, to say the very least. I decided to give in and wear my purple shirt with those three large letters across my chest. It was move-in day, after all.

New York City traffic was the definition of horrid. What should've been a forty-minute ride from home ended up taking double the time with most of that time being spent crawling through the city. I took the time to let it all sink in–this would be what I would see when I walked outside of what would be home for the next few years. I looked at the little cafes as well as the tall buildings that we drove by. Greenwich Village was so different from Long Island. I felt so many things at once, but nervousness and excitement were what I felt the most.

When we got to the apartment building, there were already a few cars unloading. We double-parked, and Mom stayed in the car as Dad and I started loading his wagon contraption. The family we had pulled up next to seemed to have just finished unpacking. This apartment building was not a NYU student housing building, but maybe they had the same idea I did. Who wants to be crammed in a tight dorm room with a bunch of loud roommates and neighbors for close to the same amount as rent for a studio? Not me. It took a lot of convincing for Mom and Dad to let me live off-campus for my first year. I had never lived on my own before, so I understood their concern. But then there was the price of rent. When I said I would work hard during the summer to put the first two months down on rent, they were happy to oblige. I was originally going to say the first three months, but I knew they had it. They wanted me to "appreciate the fruits of my labor". I got it, but with Dad being a plastic surgeon and Mom being a pediatrician, I knew they could afford it. I wouldn't have asked if I knew they couldn't. I wasn't the one who asked for a lot anyway. That was Rachel.

I could tell the young guy was a student with the small NYU letters on the right of his chest. He gave me a small nod when he spotted my shirt. I didn't know whether to smile or nod back. Bad at those things, I gave an awkward smile and turned back to Rachel, who was talking to me about an upcoming party while she pulled a suitcase toward her from the trunk.

I took the first trip upstairs with two of my bins rolling behind me on Dad's wagon. When I got to room 306, I opened the door to a small studio apartment. There was a little kitchen in one corner facing a large window. The door to the bathroom was next to the front door. It was proportional to the smallness of everything else. There was a bed frame by the wall that had a large window. The whole place wasn't much bigger than my bedroom at home, but it was my first step in being a free adult.

"This is cute," Rachel said, rolling two suitcases behind her.

"I think so too." I smiled, looking around proud.

"So, you're going to cook and actually *adult*," Rachel said, using the word as a verb instead of a noun. She got that from me, and it made me chuckle. I was going to miss living right down the hall from her.

"I guess I'll cook whenever I'm not on campus," I said.

"I'll have to come by and chill here," Rachel said, wagging her eyebrows.

"If you call in advance, and I say yes." I rolled my eyes, but really, I liked the sound of that. I knew I would miss her.

Rachel stayed in the apartment so I could go downstairs and bring more stuff up. I walked to the elevator and pressed the button. I waited, but became distracted when I heard steps walking up the stairs. I figured it was Mom or Dad when I saw the guy from the other family open the stairway door. He was tall and lean. I hadn't noticed how the purple of his shirt looked so nice next to his caramel skin before. He walked over in a confident, yet friendly, stroll.

"Hey," he said.

"Hi." I smiled shyly. I wasn't good at talking to people I didn't know.

"Are you a student too? At NYU, I mean?" he asked, returning a friendly smile, clearly not nervous at all.

"Yeah… What are you studying?" I asked.

"Pre-law." He nodded proudly.

"That's cool. I'm studying Bio." I shrugged.

The elevator pinged loudly, and the door opened. We jumped a little at the sound.

"Would you like some help moving in, um...?" he asked.

"Nicole, and sure, I guess," I said.

He ran in the elevator before it closed and then it was silent. I didn't want to stare at him, so I looked down. He was tapping his worn converse on the floor. It seemed like it was taking longer than forever when it opened. We walked outside and over to Dad. He had a few boxes by his feet.

"Hey, Dad. This is…," I trailed off and looked at the guy standing beside me, when I realized I hadn't asked for his name.

"Jason… Nice to meet you, sir." The guy smiled confidently and reached out a hand to shake with my Dad.

"Yeah. Jason is going to help bring stuff up," I said.

"Nice to meet you, Jason. What are you studying?" Dad nodded, shaking Jason's hand.

"Pre-law," he said, picking up a box.

"Oh, so you want to be a lawyer. What kind?" Dad asked as we walked back to the elevator.

"I'm not entirely sure yet. I might start with criminal law and eventually go into government… we'll see." He shrugged with a box between his arms.

We crammed into the elevator. Dad stood between Jason and I, so at least I wasn't pressed against someone I didn't know. When we got out, I led the way to my apartment. Rachel was sitting in the middle of the floor looking down at her cell phone.

"What took you so long? I have plans with… ooo hello there." She stopped and gawked at Jason. *Oh boy.*

"Hey. What's up," Jason said casually, putting down his box and grabbing the one from my arms.

"I'm fabulous. What's your name?" she asked, walking over to him, despite the look Dad was giving her.

"Jason, and yours?" Jason chuckled.

"Rachel." She flipped her freshly blown-out hair over her shoulder.

"Rachel, why don't you come downstairs and help me with the last round of boxes," Dad said with annoyance in his tone.

"Fine." Rachel rolled her eyes before dragging her feet behind him.

I saw Dad put his arm around her and kiss her forehead before the door closed. He could never stay upset with her for long. After all, they were very much alike in the way they joked around.

When they had left, Jason looked at me with a knowing smile which made me a little nervous because he didn't know me at all. I figured it was because he knew Rachel thought he was cute, but still, it made me fidget. I decided to open one of my plastic bins. I grabbed some hangers to put in the closet. I just needed to not look back at him awkwardly and *seem* awkward.

"So where are you from?" he asked after the silence had become uncomfortable… for me probably not him.

"Long Island… how about you?" I asked as I looked over my shoulder.

"Jersey," he said before walking over to my window.

"Oh… so this is probably a big change for you," I said, referring to being in the city as opposed to the quiet of Jersey he was probably used to.

"I'm from Hoboken, so it's not too different for me. I was here in the city all the time. Were you from a super quiet part of Long Island?" he asked, walking over to hand me some hangers.

"No, not super quiet, but definitely quieter than this. I'm from Lake Success, so I'm used to taking the train out here to hang out. I know the city." I finally turned to see him looking at me.

Jason is really cute, I thought. It wasn't in your devilishly handsome-might get me in trouble type of way, but in a cute, nerdy way. He had an intellectual look- if that's a thing.

"I think that's everything," Dad said after setting my mattress onto its box spring.

"Thanks, Dad," I said, hugging him.

"You're welcome baby," he said warmly.

"Thanks, Jason," I said as he stood there awkwardly.

"No problem. I should get going… I'll see you around, Nicole. It was nice meeting you guys," he said before leaving, closing the door behind him gently.

"He's so hot. God bless his genes," Rachel said.

"You made it pretty obvious that you thought so," I said.

"There are some guys that need to know that their face is delicious, and he's one of them," Rachel said.

"Alright, enough, please," Dad said, rubbing his eyes underneath his glasses.

Rachel and I giggled. Dad never liked it when Rachel mentioned guys. Despite her being seventeen, she was still the baby. On the other hand, I didn't mention guys often. I hadn't dated in two years, which seemed like forever for people my age. Rachel dated around a lot. She was the definition of a free spirit, and I think Mom and Dad had given up on trying to make her the calm kid I was. I always thought it made her fun and part of me always believed they felt the same way.

Dad and I said our goodbyes before he switched with Mom so she could see the apartment. She got teary-eyed when it was time to go. In reality, it was no big deal. I could easily take a train home and be there in an hour, but I knew it was more than that. This was the first time she had to let go.

"Come home whenever you want," she said.

"I'll come by in a few weeks," I said, kissing her on the cheek.

The apartment was too quiet when it was just me. I turned on some music on my laptop and decorated the apartment. I danced around the apartment as I put things in their place. I hung up my clothes and then put sheets on my bed. I unwrapped a few plates Mom bought me, so I had something to eat on and placed them in the cabinet above the sink.

I looked around and realized how bare all the walls were. I grabbed my tape and hung up a few posters. I started with my Coldplay poster that I had gotten signed when I was in middle school. I smiled as I put my prized possession on the wall. Then I put up my Beyoncé poster along with my poster of Aaliyah. Dad had given the latter to me. He had always said I would've loved the 90s, but I missed it by a couple of years. I always told him that that was partially his fault. He made up for it with my middle name. It was our joke. I smiled and started to miss him. I sighed inwardly. It had only been a couple of hours. *What would I do for the next few weeks until I went home*, I thought.

All of a sudden, I heard a knock on my door. I saw Jason in the peephole and opened the door.

"Hi," I said.

"Hey... I was wondering if you wanted to grab food with me tonight," Jason said with a smirk.

"Umm… what did you have in mind?" I asked, uncomfortably laughing at the extremely loud "Doo Wop" by Lauryn Hill blasting from behind me.

"I was thinking we could just look around and then decide… and get better acquainted." He shrugged.

Part of me wanted to say no. I promised myself that I would not get involved with boys this semester. At the same time, I didn't want to not have a social life. Making friends was definitely a must.

"Yeah sure. Can you give me a few minutes?" I asked.

"Yeah! I'll wait. Take all the time you need," he said.

I smiled awkwardly and closed the door. I turned off my music and then ran to the bathroom. I made sure my box braids were parted the way I liked them and then I dabbed the shininess from the hot summer day from my nose. I put on some lip gloss and grabbed my little crossbody before opening the door again. Jason was leaning against the wall across from the door looking at his phone. He looked up at me and gave me a small smile.

"All ready?" he asked.

"Yeah," I said back.

"The world is our oyster or whatever they say when one goes off to college," Jason said, mockingly stretching his arms out as if he was saying "ta-da".

"Something like that." I chuckled as we got in the elevator.

We decided on a pizza parlor a few blocks away from the apartment building. Its vibe was relaxed with jazzy music playing and signed photos of stars on the wall. The booth was comfortable, and it felt clean. It was set right by a window, and I happily watched people walk by—all either starting, continuing, or ending chapters of their own.

"So… Are we going to do the shy and cute thing all night or…," Jason said with his mouth half full. I would've usually been disgusted, but for some reason, I was amused as well as intrigued by his need to get words out right then and there.

"What?" I asked, chuckling, trying not to choke.

"I don't know. I'm getting shy vibes from you," he said.

"Well that vibe reading is inaccurate," I answered dryly.

Jason's eyebrows raised at that, and I laughed in response. He smiled, and I looked down immediately because I was not going to think about how cute he was. I just kept repeating the word *friend* in my head. I looked up and saw that look. It was the look guys that were too cute for their own good got when they were openly checking a girl out. It always made me somewhat self-conscious. I guessed I looked okay. My hair had just been braided a few days before, I had that summer glow still going on which made my skin look extra healthy… I couldn't complain.

"Ok fine, so tell me more about yourself. Maybe I can get a better impression," he said.

"What do you want to know?" I asked. I hated being asked that. I never knew what to say.

"What's your favorite movie?"

"That's hard. I like different movies for different reasons… I guess I would have to say *Dead Poets Society* or *Good Will Hunting*," I answered.

"Interesting. You like Robin Williams," he said as a statement, but I guessed it was a question.

"Who doesn't? He was funny and an amazing actor," I said.

"Agreed. I'd have to say I'm between *Gone with the Wind* or *Love Jones*," he said, leaning back like he was thinking hard.

"Very different movies," I said.

"Yeah, but I just like *Gone with the Wind* 'cause the last line is great "Frankly, my dear, I don't give a damn." All this pomp and circumstance and that's how it ends. It's funny. *Love Jones* 'cause of what it means to my family," he said with a smile.

"What does it mean?" I asked, hoping he was willing to share.

"My Dad is a white guy from a part of town that didn't have a lot of people who looked like my mom. He wasn't sure how to get her to take him seriously, so he recited a poem like one of those cool ones in the movie. She laughed so hard, and I guess the rest is history," he said, and I could see his love for them in his eyes.

"That's ridiculously cute," I said in between giggling at the thought.

He said something under his breath, but I couldn't hear it.

"What?" I asked.

"Nothing. So, what made you decide on studying Biology?" he asked.

"I always wanted to become a doctor, I guess. My parents are both doctors. They help so many people… I just want to do that too," I said.

"So, does that mean I get, like, free surgeries and stuff?" he asked with a smirk.

"We'll see…" I rolled my eyes and laughed.

"Wrong answer. Nicole, you already got your license taken away before you even got it," he teased.

"What a shame," I deadpanned with a chuckle.

Chapter 3

I expected my first day of class to be different, but instead, it was actually one of the most boring things I had ever experienced. Why did we need to read the syllabi together? We were in college. It was certain we knew how to read and how to refer to the syllabus, just like we did in high school. Every professor would go over their syllabus like it was something special; like it wasn't like all the others. I took it all in stride, though. I was starting a new chapter, and I was happy to be in my dream school. *Not every story hits the ground running*, I reminded myself.

Jason and I had been hanging out almost everyday since I moved in. On the elevator that morning, he asked to meet me for lunch. Instead of the Italian restaurant near the apartment that we had fallen in love with, we decided to explore the options on campus. We met in one of the buildings' food courts to eat. I walked in, and before I knew it, Jason was standing by my side as we decided between tacos or Asian stir fry.

"How was it?" Jason asked, playfully nudging my arm.

"What?" I asked.

"Your first day of classes," he said.

"Pretty good. I met a couple people. It was a little boring, though. We just read the syllabi in both of the classes, so there was nothing new learned or anything." I shrugged.

"Same here, but I'm sure they'll throw the load of work on really soon. I somehow got convinced to join the debate team, so that's how my afternoon is going to go," he said.

I didn't answer. There was a guy who looked so familiar standing near us, looking around. It was just the back of his head that I could mostly see, but I was pretty sure I had seen that head of dark wavy hair and those broad shoulders before. He turned to the side and my stomach fell. I felt like I was going down a roller coaster at that very second, one that was nowhere close to being over. I shook my head and took a step back in disbelief.

"So, there's this party going on tonight... I was wondering if you'd like to go with me?" Jason asked.

I glanced at Jason, but I couldn't answer. I was too in shock and my brain was everywhere but in the mindset to be thinking about a party. My body reacted, specifically my lungs, before my brain did. It took forever for me to even catch my breath.

"Noah, what are you doing here?" I asked the guy standing just a few feet from us.

He turned around slowly. I saw that familiar sharp jawline, now dusted with a new small shadow of hair. When those mysterious green eyes met mine, I knew for sure it was my ex-boyfriend.

He just stared for a moment, and I did the same back. It was like we were doing that thing people do when they hadn't seen each other in a long time—looking to see what was different and what was the same. Although, those are usually under much happier circumstances. This, undoubtedly, was not. There wasn't much different about Noah Crawford, but it had been a couple years. He looked older, but he was still Noah. He was built like an athlete and had chiseled features that cut the way light hit his face. His eyes always looked at you like he knew your secrets. Noah slid his hands into his front pockets and leaned back on his heels as he looked at me. It was way too familiar for someone who hadn't seen me in years. I narrowed my eyes in response.

"Hey Nikki…" Noah finally said with a small smile.

"What are you doing here?" I repeated.

"I go here," he said softly.

I shook my head violently. This was not happening. He had to be kidding—not that this was in any way, shape, or form funny. Either way, it had to be a joke because I was *not* going to let this happen.

"No no no no… No, you don't." My finger wagged in disgust.

"Yes, I do," Noah said, pressing his full lips together into a firm line.

Jason cleared his throat at that. I had forgotten he was there. Noah's eyes shifted from me to him. He gave him a thoughtful look before he looked back at me. I looked over my shoulder at Jason, who was starting to take a few steps back.

"I'll just catch you later, Nicole," Jason said before disappearing into the sea of students walking around. All I could do was watch him leave. My head was too hyper-focused on the person in front of me to respond.

"How was I supposed to know you go here," Noah said, addressing my sour expression as he brought my attention back to him.

"You… I… whatever," I stumbled.

It was silent for a while. I was processing what he said. He was right. Thousands of people went to this school. There was no way he could've known I would go here. What would the point of that be anyway? I sighed miserably when I realized this was not going to end up how I wanted it, and a little because of how insane I sounded. There was no point trying to argue and make a point when I was in a state of shock anyway.

"You… look good. How have you been?" Noah asked with a shy smile.

"I don't want to talk to you," I spat back.

"Nicole, don't do this," he said, staring back at me in the eyes.

"Don't do what?" I rolled my eyes.

"Be angry… this isn't you," he said softly.

"You know what also isn't me, Noah?" I asked as my head started to hurt.

He paused at that and his eyes widened just a little. I pressed my lips together as I tried to hold down the lump I could feel in my throat. I was also trying to hold back the memories. I didn't want to go back to that day, but I was.

***

I walked to Noah's house like I always did on summer afternoons. I was always the first one up, and sometimes, by the time I got there, he was still asleep. Ms. Crawford would be downtown at the office by then, so I would be the one to wake him. I remembered that day being different. It felt different. Something kept telling me not to leave the house, but I did anyway.

I walked up to Noah's door and opened it with the spare key he had hidden for me. It was almost always unlocked, but this time it wasn't. Then, it was like time had stopped. It was as if my brain couldn't process the image I was looking at. The only noise that could leave my lips was a gasp. Before I knew it, a hand was pulling me into the house and slamming the door closed. Noah's white t-shirt was covered in the same thing that was pooling on the floor —blood. Right in the middle of it, his uncle—his father's brother, Reggie. His lifeless body lay there in the middle of the foyer.

"What the hell happened? What did you do? Is he... is he dead?" I stammered, trying to formulate a sentence.

"Nicole——" he just said.

I didn't answer. I couldn't. All I could do was look at the scene in front of me. His body laid face down on the floor. The blood made a drastic contrast against the white marble tiles. It was horrific, but I couldn't look away.

"Nicole, look at me," he repeated, grabbing my arm this time.

"Is he dead? Answer me right now," I demanded, even though, deep down, I already knew the answer.

"Yes… Nicole, look at me," he said.

I slowly turned to him. I was starting to put things together in my head. I could feel goosebumps rise on my arm. My stomach was a mess.

"You killed him?" I asked, taking a step back.

"He is dead," he said, not answering my question.

"That is not what I asked you! Did you kill him?" I screamed.

"Yes, Nicole! Are you happy now? Yes, I did," he bellowed back, making me take another step back.

I just stared at him for a moment, holding my breath, mainly because I was in shock but also to hold back my breakfast that was coming up. How could *my* Noah do something like this? He was the most gentle guy I knew.

"But why?" I asked, but it came out super small.

"He tried to kill my mother." His voice shook.

"Oh my God. No. Noah… you…" I tried to make sense of what I wanted to say.

"I need you to go home." He let out a deep sigh.

"What are you going to do? This is crazy. You have to call someone," I said, patting my back pocket for my phone.

"No! Are you kidding me? No... stop," he said, jumping toward me and grabbing my phone.

"What are you going to do, Noah? You can't just act like this didn't happen," I said.

"No. You didn't see a thing. If they ask, I need you to tell them you weren't here," he said sternly.

"Tell who? What? Who is *"they"*? What are you talking about?" I shook my head trying to get everything to stop spinning for just one moment.

"The cops," he said.

"You want me to lie? I can't lie. They'll know. Oh my God. I will go to jail too. We—" I began to panic.

"Nicole! Focus! You need to focus. We don't have time! Please." Noah shook me, fear in his eyes and voice.

***

I hadn't realized I was reliving the moment while staring at Noah until he took a step near me. My reflexes made me jump back right into a guy carrying a cup. The drink sloshed out the sides and onto his hand.

"Oh, sorry," I said. The sound of defeat in my voice matched my mood to a T.

"Uh yeah... don't worry about it," the guy sighed before walking away.

I turned to look at Noah, who just watched. He was still just looking at me. His eyes were sad. It was as if they were able to see my thoughts and couldn't help but feel bad for me. It made me beyond uncomfortable. I didn't want his pity.

"I'm sorry. I don't know what to say," Noah finally said.

He was right. There was nothing left to say. What could he say? Sorry for screwing you up? Sorry for the nightmares that you have way too many times to admit? There was nothing he could do to fix this. To fix me.

"There isn't anything else to say, Noah," I said before walking away.

Did I mention I hate surprises?

Chapter 4

Nineteen hours. That's how long it had been since I had last slept. Every few minutes, I had to remind myself to not tense my jaw, to unclench my fists. I couldn't stop the shaking or the crying. I just had to deal with that. I looked at the clock to see how much time had passed, but none did. It was still one in the morning.

I looked at my bathroom door and thought about the medicine cabinet in the bathroom. I thought about taking one of those little pills. It would help, and I could finally sleep. It had been a year since I actually took one. Of course, there were times when I thought about taking it, but I had been able to get past it using the techniques Dr. Harris taught me. This was different. It had been the first time I had seen Noah since he had left. I could hardly process what I was feeling, let alone even think about trying to calm down about it.

***

Noah sat in my desk chair with a tired expression. We had been doing this for hours. I had finally been able to speak without crying. It had been an excruciatingly long day.

"So where were you again?" he asked in a professional tone.

"Um… I went to get ice cream," I struggled.

"You rode your bike to get ice cream with your friends," he said.

"Right. I rode my bike to get ice cream with my friends," I repeated.

"Would Noah ever kill anyone?" he asked.

I was silent. My head hurt. All I wanted to do was take a nap, or even better, wake up from this nightmare. Having to look at the boy I was so unequivocally in love with and know he did something so inexcusable did things that I still have no words to describe. Noah reached out and tried to grab my hand. I pulled back. It had been a reflex for the past week, and I didn't know how to get better. Every time I did, Noah looked physically pained, which just made everything hurt more.

"We're almost done… I'm sorry Nikki," he said softly.

"No. He would never," I said, ignoring his last statement.

I really was over hearing him apologize. It didn't help anything. It didn't help my restless nights or stop me from reaching for the bat underneath my bed every time I heard noises at night. *Sorry* was just a word that made me feel even worse about the whole thing.

"Did he kill Reggie?" Noah asked in a low voice.

"No. He loves his family," I said, feeling half-dead.

We heard a knock on my closed door before it opened. Mom and Dad were standing there with grave looks on their faces. They didn't even mention the door being closed. They felt the stress of the situation too. The press had gotten out of hand, and every day my parents got home, they would be stopped by reporters.

"It's getting late, you two," Dad said.

Noah nodded and looked over at me. He leaned in for a kiss, but I moved so he got my cheek instead. He shut his eyes tightly for a moment before he left. I knew that hurt him, but I was hurting too. I hysterically cried myself to sleep that night, and for many nights after. That was one of the last times I saw him before he left town.

***

My eyes fell on the books that sat by the kitchenette. I had a day full of class in a few hours. I needed to sleep. I sighed in defeat and walked to the bathroom.

I decided to conform to the ways of my fellow students and hang out in the park after class. I had not been up to socializing the few days before then, but I felt much better and was ready to somewhat face the world, more than just going to class. I found a bench and sat down. I felt awkward sitting alone, so I took my laptop out and tried to look busy.

"I missed you the past couple of days. You ok, Smith?" a voice asked, startling me.

I looked up to see Jason in a polo, his messenger bag hanging across his lean body. His sunglasses sat on the bridge of his freckled nose. His curly hair looked perfectly tousled. I realized I had been staring for too long when he tilted his head after a moment. *Oh, he's waiting for me to answer*, I remembered. Good job, Nicole.

"Yeah… just busy." I shrugged.

"Mind if I sit?" he asked, briefly tilting his sunglasses up to show his eyes.

"Sure," I said, sliding over a little.

"So, now that we're friends," he began after sitting down.

"We're friends?" I asked as I chuckled.

"Absolutely. Anyway, since we're *best* friends—" he started again.

"Wow, that was fast."

"Quite, but who was that guy? Your ex?"

"Oh… Um yeah, Noah and I dated a couple years ago," I answered, not needing to clarify because I knew who he was asking about.

Jason waited quietly behind his sunglasses. He was waiting for me to say more. Unfortunately for him, I was not in the mood for story time.

"How did you know he was my ex?" I asked.

"When you saw him, it's like you saw an ax murderer," he said.

"Wait what?" My heart stopped, and I almost dropped my laptop.

"Shit, dude, relax… I'm just saying you looked pretty shaken up when you saw him. Did it end badly?" he asked.

I did not want to talk about Noah. I had spent the past few days thinking about him, and I was over it.

"It's really complicated. I hope I don't see him around. I don't need that right now. I need only good vibes right now… and language," I said.

"Oh sorry… Good for you, but don't look 'cause he's headed this way," Jason said, looking over my shoulder.

I gasped really loudly, which made Jason's expression turn from relaxed to completely amused. His eyebrows went up from behind his sunglasses and the corner of his lip went up. Since we were *best friends* now, would it be cool for me to smack him? I really wanted to smack him for laughing at my misery. My heart started to race.

"Hide me," I blurted out.

"He clearly has already seen you." Jason chuckled.

"Ok, then let's leave," I said, grabbing my stuff.

"He's like ten feet away," Jason said in a hushed tone.

"Fuck," I whispered back.

"*Language*," Jason whispered with a fake shocked expression that would've made me laugh if it were any other time.

All of a sudden, I felt someone standing over us. Jason and I stared at each other for a moment frozen. It was clear neither one of us knew what to do at that moment. Jason looked away first and gave Noah a nod.

"Nicole, can we talk for a sec?" Noah asked. I knew it was his voice before I even looked.

"I'm busy right now," I said, finally looking up at him.

"I could go," Jason offered as he stood up.

"No, you don't have—" I began.

"That would be great. Thanks man," Noah cut me off.

"Noah, seriously? We have nothing to talk about," I sighed and rubbed my temples.

"Well, I'm gonna let you guys have this *convo* about nothing… see ya," Jason said with a look that looked amused and sorry at the same time.

I glared at my new *best friend,* who flashed me a forced smile as he backed up. He shrugged apologetically before turning around and walking away. My eyes shifted to Noah, who was watching us. I couldn't read his expression.

"Who's he… Do I know him?" Noah asked in an annoyed tone.

Of all the things I had been preparing myself for him to say, that was not one of them. I just stared at him for a moment. Was he serious? We had stopped dating two whole years ago. *He should expect me to be dating, or even have another boyfriend, by now*, I thought. Also, he did not know everyone I knew anymore. It had been, and I hope you've been following along thus far, two years!

"You are impossible," I said as I picked up my stuff to leave.

"No, I'm sorry. Wait," he said as he put his hands out for me to stop.

I stopped what I was doing and looked at him. He had thirty seconds to convince me to listen to him, or I was going to go home right that moment, order take-out, and cry over how messy my life was. Screw outside.

"I don't want it to be like this between us, Nikki," he breathed.

"How the hell do you want it to be, Noah? This is your fault," I said, zipping up my bag.

"I want us to be friends… I guess," he drifted off because, like me, I'm sure he realized how dumb of an idea that was.

I stopped and stared at Noah again. He had to be kidding me. He had put me through hell, and I let him because I loved him. I knew I did. It wasn't one of those relationships you looked back at and laughed because you knew it wasn't as serious as you once thought. No, Noah and I were different. I knew I loved him with everything in me. He was my world. Then I realized I clearly wasn't his when he made me commit a crime to cover his butt and then left suddenly.

"Friends? No. Not after everything." I crossed my arms.

"Can we talk somewhere private? I can explain," he said.

"Do I look like I was born yesterday to you? Absolutely not," I said, putting my bag on my shoulder and starting to walk away.

Before I knew it, I felt a firm grip on my arm. It wasn't forceful, but it wasn't playful either. If it were anyone else, I would've pulled away and screamed at them for doing that, but this was Noah. I looked up at him and glared. His eyes were already on mine and giving me that look. It made me angry, but it was something I could almost never resist. He gave me that look that meant he was serious. Something was wrong. I could tell from his eyes.

"I just want to talk. I promise you that is all I want," he said, even though his eyes clearly said something different.

"Fine. Where?" I sighed.

Chapter 5

Noah and I walked to his dorm building a couple blocks away from the park. He insisted what he had to say had to be somewhere completely private. I didn't like the idea of going to his dorm, but I didn't disagree about keeping whatever he had to say between us only. There was too much dangerous history.

The dorm building was much less quiet than my apartment building. Students were talking in the halls, and the sound of music came from an unknown source. There was something really nice about it, but I wondered if I would appreciate it all if it were my reality every day. My assumption was probably not. I know what you're thinking, and the answer is yes, I only had so much tolerance for those of my generation. I played it off like I did, though. Most people had no idea.

"This is me," Noah said as he finally stopped at a door.

"I shouldn't have even agreed to this. Being alone with you is dangerous," I said.

Noah turned around with a smirk. I *did not* mean that in the good way. I looked up at the ceiling as I prayed for a morsel of patience.

"Because you have *literally* proven yourself to be dangerous. Don't get excited," I said.

He deflated a little as he took out his ID card and unlocked it. He stepped aside for me to walk in. Inside looked a lot like a regular apartment, but a little smaller than the one I lived in. He only had a microwave and refrigerator. There was a window, a little closet, and then a bed.

"Would you like something to drink? Tea? I know you love your tea. Unless you don't anymore… Orange juice, maybe?" Noah asked as he opened up his little refrigerator.

"No, thanks though," I said curtly before leaning on the wall furthest from him.

Noah just stared at me for the next few moments. I couldn't read his expression this time.

"What? Why are you staring at me like that?" I finally asked uneasily.

"Nothing. You're just really beautiful," Noah said with an honest smile.

I rolled my eyes. I did not return the favor of complimenting him back like I usually did in a situation like this. Instead, I gave him an incredulous look. He couldn't be serious. I tossed my braids over my shoulder and crossed my arms. I was not going to melt over his kind words like I used to.

"That's not why we're here," I sighed, already done with this conversation before it even started.

"Right. I guess I'll just pull it off like a band-aid," he breathed.

"Go for it," I answered sarcastically.

"I didn't do it," he said, stuffing his hands in his pockets.

"You… didn't do what?" I asked, confused.

"I… didn't kill Reggie. It wasn't me," he said.

"Oh right, so why did you… why did *we* go through all of that for nothing?" I asked.

"I had to cover for someone else," he said.

My head started to hurt a little. I did not want to hear any of this. Everything that I thought was the truth, and had finally come to terms with, was now being rushed out from under me. What was the point of Noah lying? Not even to the cops, but to me? It didn't make sense.

"Nikki, I couldn't kill a man if I tried. You know me," he added softly after I didn't answer for a while.

Noah took a step toward me, but I pressed myself firmly against the wall. I couldn't trust him. He lied to me. He made me lie to myself and everyone I loved.

"Noah… if you're lying to me, just stop," I finally said, rubbing my temples.

"I am not lying to you," he said, taking a step in my direction. I put my hand out immediately.

"Then who did it?" I asked, not convinced just yet.

He went silent at that. His jaw looked tight, and his hands shook just a little. I wasn't sure what I believed, but I knew I wanted to hear his answer. I could feel the goosebumps rising on my arm.

"I… I can't tell you," he said under his breath.

His eyes met mine, and for a moment, they looked so afraid. I almost felt bad for him. Then I remembered it could all be a lie. I closed my eyes for a moment as I tried to process it all.

"I just thought you should know," he said.

"Why… who–" were the only words that came out as my brain tried to make some sense of this.

"It's complicated… I already said enough. I just wanted you to know it's not me," he said quickly, showing just how nervous he was.

"Why didn't you tell me?" I asked.

"You would cover for me, but you would never cover for… who did it," he said.

"I don't know about all of that," I argued.

Noah looked at me through furrowed brows as he crossed his arms. We both knew he was right. I was not the biggest fan of his family, especially when it came to his mother. It's not that I didn't like Tracey; it's that we never were on the best of terms because she didn't think I was good enough for her son. Noah always told me it had nothing to do with the color of my skin, but I was never fully convinced. I mean, it was debatable that the woman may have rather me dead than date her only child. Either way, I could never imagine Tracey Crawford bothering herself enough to chip a nail let alone kill someone. I guess it was someone else, but who? *If this was even true in the first place*, I thought.

"Fine," I said as I rolled my eyes.

"Anyway, I just wanted you to know that," he said, rubbing the back of his neck.

"And why, after two years, do you just trust me enough to throw that information around?" I asked.

"Because you may not think so, but I know you," Noah said.

I shook my head because I had no idea what else to do. Part of me didn't want to know because knowing made me feel like an accomplice. I mean, in reality, I already was. The other part was partially relieved to hear that this could be the truth. It made things hurt less. Though, I couldn't help but still wonder. There had been so much evidence pointing to Noah, but if he didn't do it, then why?

"Why did you leave?" I asked.

"Tracey thought it would be best," he said.

"Since when do you call your mom by her first name?" I asked.

"Since she stopped being who I thought she was," Noah answered.

I took a long shower that night. In my mind, I hoped that all the water would wash away my thoughts and discoveries from the day. It didn't work, but it definitely made me feel better. My phone played music, and the shower kept me warm as I tried my best to unwind for the weekend. I knew the song by heart, but it was like I could hear an extra beat that was not there. I thought I might've imagined it, but then it happened again and again. I realized someone was knocking on the front door.

I turned off the water and quickly did a terrible job of drying myself before pulling on my big t-shirt over my bun of braids. Then I threw on some shorts. I took a long look at myself in the mirror. I frowned at how young my fresh face looked. I walked over to the front door and looked through the peephole. It was Jason with his laptop resting on top of a box of pizza. I laughed inwardly. The sight summed him up perfectly. He was always working and always eating. I opened the door.

"Hi," I said.

"Hey, Smith! You mind if I come in?" Jason said, raising his laptop and pizza.

"Yeah… I mean, no, I don't mind. I just wasn't expecting anyone," I said as I fanned my shirt. I was still super hot from the shower.

"Why are you sweating so much? Are you good?" Jason asked.

"I was taking a shower. It's water… mostly," I said, stepping aside and letting him in.

"Well dry off. I brought pizza. I also wanted to ask you something," Jason said, putting the box on my counter.

"Ugh," I grunted as I walked back into the bathroom and closed the door. I needed to dry off properly.

"We're best friends now. We do this shit. I expect Chinese food at my place tomorrow!" Jason chuckled from the kitchen.

I dried off properly and then started to rub cocoa butter into my skin before throwing back on my clothes. I took my time, but it was clear Jason was impatient about whatever he wanted to show me. After the third time he had asked if I was done, I walked out of the bathroom and glared at him. He gave me a big smile before dramatically putting his arm out to present the pizza.

"Thanks for the food." I chuckled softly.

"You're welcome. I aim to please." He flashed his eyebrows before sitting on the futon.

I grabbed a slice and sat near him at the foot of my bed. I nearly inhaled it. It was one of those moments you didn't realize how hungry you were until you started eating.

"What song is this?" Jason asked as my phone continued to play music in the background.

""Hymn for The Weekend" by Beyoncé and Coldplay," I said with my mouth half-full before cringing at how gross I probably sounded.

Jason just nodded and listened. He drummed his fingers on his lap and nodded his head to the beat. His eyes seemed distracted, though. I hadn't known him for long, but I had seen enough facial expressions to know something was off. He finally noticed me looking at him and grabbed my phone that was near him. The music was off in seconds.

"Yeah… I wasn't listening to that. Thanks for asking." I deadpanned.

"Can I ask you something?" he asked.

I always hated that question. It usually came before a question that I did not want to answer. If it weren't rude, I'd answer no. At least this wasn't in text so I didn't have to wait in agony.

"Yeah, I guess," I said as I pulled my legs to my chest.

Jason's eyes lingered on mine for a moment before he reached for his laptop next to him. He opened it up and turned it so the screen could face me. On the screen read a headline that read "Lake Success' Missing Man Case Gone Cold". I sighed involuntarily.

"How did you even find that?" I asked in disbelief that once again I couldn't escape this.

"I looked Noah up… it started because I just wanted to know what his deal was with not leaving you alone, but then he came up in *quite a few articles*," Jason said, turning the screen back around and looking at it with wide eyes.

I didn't know what to say. Whenever people asked me about the case, I would try to change the subject or just say that I didn't know. There was a point in time when the press surrounding it had gotten so bad, Dad had to drive me to and from school to make sure I wasn't bombarded with questions. The police were enough. Noah's family owned a huge company in the city. Money and drama seemed to be the perfect mixture for the papers.

"Yeah, it's pretty terrible. The police never found his uncle," I said.

"Your name came up too. Noah was a suspect and you two dated," he said.

"I know... I was there," I said dryly before walking into the kitchen.

"Is that why you two broke up?" Jason asked.

I gave him an annoyed look from the kitchen, and he put his hands up in defeat. I was not talking about this right now. Not only because I didn't want to, but because I knew how unpredictable my emotions were and how anxious I got whenever it was brought up. I could feel my eye starting to twitch and nothing was even happening. Jason wouldn't see that part of me after only three weeks of knowing me.

"It's an interesting case, y'know." He shrugged.

"Okay... so?" I asked.

"So... it would be cool to look into. I do need a case," he said before walking over to get another slice.

"A case for what?" I asked.

"Solving a local cold case would be amazing for my resume. It would make me stand out for law school and for other future prospects," he said.

My stomach was a mess, and more talk of this could've ended in the pizza coming right back up. I took a long swig of water as I thought about what to say next.

"I don't think there's anything else to find out. The investigation lasted forever, and they still never found anything." I shrugged.

"Maybe they just need a new set of eyes," he answered with his mouth half-full.

"I think you should look into something else," I said.

"Why do you care so much?" he asked, giving me a questioning look.

I thought for a long moment. I had to make this believable. I had to focus not on the fact that I was lying, but instead on what could happen if I didn't. I cringed at the thought. It was all too familiar to the last time I had to lie about this.

"Because it turned my town and my life upside down. I want it in the past," I said.

It was true. Life had never really been the same since it happened. Every time someone brought up Noah, my body would start to hurt. It wasn't only because he broke my heart, but because I was scared someone would ask about the case. I was scared that one slip up and I would end up behind bars; that my life would be over. Everything I worked for would be down the drain. Yes, I had lied, but there was no turning back. I had to keep this going, forever.

"Fine. I'll try to find something else," Jason sighed.

"Thanks. I appreciate it," I said with the best smile my face could conjure.

Chapter 6

The next day, Rachel stopped by without giving me prior notice, her signature. The only reason I let her in without a fight was that she brought food. I hadn't spent money on food for the past couple of meals, and I was not complaining. I was living on somewhat of a budget now. Rachel was definitely not. She had no idea what was coming once she moved out.

My sister wore a long flowing orange sundress. Her hair was pulled up into a puff on the top of her head like a crown.

"I saw Jason on my way up here," she said after we finished another episode of *Gossip Girl*.

"Good for you," I deadpanned.

She turned around slowly and looked at me with her eyebrows raised.

"What's the matter?" she asked.

"He wants to look into the Reggie Crawford case," I sighed.

Her face turned from potentially amused to a wide-eyed scared look. Rachel didn't know all the details about why it wasn't a good idea, but she had enough sense to not ask more. I was glad. I never lied to her, and she didn't deserve to be involved in it. I think it was her sister's intuition that told her that whatever had happened with Noah and myself had taken a permanent toll.

"Tell him to fuck off. You don't need to go through that drama again," she said.

"Language… and I told him that it would mean a lot to me if he didn't. He said he wasn't going to. Let's hope he's telling the truth," I sighed.

"You should keep an eye on him. I'm sure I know only half of it, but that case made the town crazy. He probably doesn't know what he's getting into. Oh Coco, like I always say, the cute ones are always dangerous," she said.

"Yeah, I guess. He's always around, so I'm sure I'd know what he's up to," I said, hugging my pillow.

"He's always around? Like here?"

"Yeah, here, and we always run into each other."

Rachel swung around to look at me dead-on. She clapped excitedly and gave a giggle that came deep from her soul.

"So, he's a potential boy," she said.

"He is a boy." I rolled my eyes.

"Nicole, you know what I mean. *He's a prospect.* He's a potential beau. I saw how he looked at you the day you moved in here." She wagged her eyebrows.

"I don't know about all of that. We're just friends right now, and … I don't know," I said.

"He doesn't want to be just friends," she sighed.

"He said we are friends," I said, rolling over to not look at her.

"That's what boys do. They are all somewhat dumb. There are just some that are more worth helping than others. He's one. His face makes up for it. Have you seen it? I have," she went on.

"Yes, he's incredibly attractive. Relax," I said, throwing my pillow at her.

"Okay fine. I'm just saying, if you need to keep him close anyway, you might as well use it to your advantage 'cause he's spicy." She laughed.

"Don't you have homework or something?" I yawned because I was both tired from this conversation and in general.

"Yeah. I'm leaving. I have a party in Queens in an hour," she said, looking at her cell phone as she got up.

"Do you ever sleep?" I asked.

"I'll sleep when I'm dead," she said as she leaned down to kiss my cheek.

"Be good." I chuckled.

"Keep me posted about Jason. Love you," she said before walking out the door.

I got to English class early and found my unassigned-assigned seat in the middle of the lecture hall. I opened my laptop and watched as my missed texts came in. There were the usual ones I got from Mom every morning, a funny meme from Michelle, and then there was a message from a number with no name assigned to it. I clicked on that first.

Unknown Number: Hey Nicole this is Noah. I'm hoping you have the same number. Do you want to grab lunch today on campus? I figured it would be nice to catch up. Something chill.

What was he doing? I sat and watched the screen for a few minutes, unable to formulate a response. Why was he reaching out all of a sudden? I hadn't seen him since he told me he didn't do it, and that was over a week ago. I hadn't completely decided whether I believed him or not. It's not like we were buddies now, but I always would have an unwelcome soft spot for Noah. I rolled my eyes as I typed "Yeah sure" on the keyboard. *Maybe he'll explain more about what he told me about the murder*, I thought. Part of me wanted to find out more for my own sanity, even though as far as the law was concerned, that was probably a bad idea. At this point, no one would really know. He responded almost instantly.

Noah Crawford: Great! How does noon sound?

I rolled my eyes at how eager he sounded. I waited a minute before I responded. My answer was much calmer.

Nicole Smith: Sounds good.

I sat in the cafeteria typing out a paper. Class had let out early, and I had some time to kill. It was better to get the paper done then because I had a biology test coming up that I would have to study for that night. I would need the quiet of my apartment for that. After being in the honors program in high school, I found that I was able to write a paper just about anywhere. I was on a roll, writing down at least fifty words a minute. My train of thought was broken when my phone started to vibrate across the table. Noah's name shone brightly on the screen, and I picked it up.

"Hi," I answered.

"Is that you sitting down by the window?" Noah asked, which made me start to look around the room.

"Um… yeah. Where are you?" I asked.

"In the line for burgers. Are you down for that? I could bring it over to you," Noah offered on the other side of the line.

"You sure? I'll pay you back then," I said.

"No worries. Cheeseburger with fries and… no tomatoes, but you want pickles, right? Do you still like it like that?" he asked.

My heart fell a little. He remembered. And the fact that he did hurt more than made me feel good. All the memories of how good things were before started to seep in my mind. I began to wonder if this lunch meeting was a good idea.

"That's perfect," I said, more sadly than I intended to sound.

"Okay cool. I'll be over in ten," Noah said before hanging up.

I cleared my throat and opened my eyes wide so the tears would fall back. This was not the time to start crying. I didn't even know why I was crying. Noah would be sitting across from me in just a few short minutes. I distracted myself by looking up Noah's Cash-Me username and sent him $6 for the meal. I didn't want to owe him anything, and this was definitely not a date. Then I typed a few more thoughts in the document my paper was in before I noticed a tall shadow standing over the table. I looked up to see Noah standing there with a tray full of food. He had a small smile on his face.

"Hey," I said, sliding my books over to make space.

"Someone looks busy," he said.

"Yeah, but I'm managing well. I'm just doing this now so I can study for my first bio test tonight," I said, putting the books back in my bag one by one.

"Is that your major?" he asked, finally sitting down.

"Yeah. What's yours?" I asked.

I always knew I wanted to be a doctor. I used to put bandages on my stuffed animals. In high school, I would take all the science electives possible. Noah was different. He was good at a lot of things. He wasn't sure what he wanted to do. One time it was film, another it was being a physical therapist, and the last thing we spoke about before we broke up was him becoming a teacher. He could do anything he put his mind to.

"Psychology. I'm really into the mind and how people think," he said.

"That's cool. Do you know what you want to do with that yet?" I asked.

"Maybe helping people in a mental hospital... I don't know. We'll see." He shrugged.

I nodded and continued eating. There was an awkward silence between us for a little bit. We both looked out the window, at the students walking by, and wherever else that didn't require each other. I just felt awkward, but Noah looked like he had been thinking.

"So how has your life been? Anything new?" Noah finally asked, breaking the awkward silence and making it even weirder.

"Nothing really," I said.

"I'm sure there's something... *someone*." He smiled, but it didn't reach his eyes.

I knew what he was trying to ask. He was trying to ask if I was seeing anyone. The answer was no, but he didn't have to know that I hadn't dated anyone since we broke up. I was quickly calculating the perfect way to change the subject when I caught Jason walking up to us at the corner of my eye. *Of course.*

"Hey, you two," Jason said, and I could hear the amusement in his voice.

"Look who it is," Noah said, clearly annoyed.

"How's your day going?" Jason said.

I could tell the question was geared toward me, but he glanced at Noah, too, to be polite. Noah stared at Jason as he pulled up a chair to sit with us. He had that thoughtful look he always had when he was trying to figure something out. His eyes finally slid over to mine. His eyebrows raised a little as if he came to some conclusion in his mind. I narrowed my eyes to question his look, but instead, he turned back to Jason.

"My day was good. Went to the gym and then class," Noah said.

"What *is your major*, Noah? I don't think I ever got the chance to ask," Jason said, opening up his container revealing a healthy amount of pasta with pesto on top.

Noah's eyes fell back on me again. I was still mostly focusing on him. I was trying to figure out what was running through his mind. *What was with the knowing look*, I thought. He leaned back in his seat before his eyes went back to Jason.

"Psychology, and you?" Noah asked before going back to eating his food.

"Pre-law," Jason said.

"Ah good ole' pre-law," Noah said in the friendliest way he could say it possible, but I could tell from his eyes that he was being sarcastic.

"Yeah. You have an interest in it, too?" Jason asked with an innocent glint in his eyes.

"No, it's not my thing. My father always had a joke about lawyers." Noah smirked with a mischievous look in his eyes.

Noah never really spoke about his father. Carter Crawford had passed away when Noah was twelve. I hadn't met Noah yet when it happened, but when we started dating, he would simply say "that day changed everything". Noah and I spoke about nearly everything, but things with his family were very off-limits for him, and I respected that. Not everybody had a good relationship with their parents. I wasn't able to relate to that, and I never tried.

"What's the difference between a cactus and a courtroom?" Noah asked.

Jason's eyebrows furrowed for a moment before he glanced over at me. I also did not know the answer. I just shrugged before looking at Noah with a wide-eyed *please behave* look.

"Hmm, I don't know. What?" Jason asked.

"On a cactus, the pricks are on the outside," Noah said.

Jason's face was blank for a moment. His eyes narrowed just a bit before his smile returned. He forced a laugh out before giving me an unamused look. I looked over at Noah, who triumphantly bit into his burger. The wondering was over. I knew this lunch meeting was a bad idea.

Chapter 7

Coming home for the first weekend since I started school was a weird experience. I had never not felt at home, at home, but I did this time. I had gotten so used to the apartment that it took me a while to get comfortable in my room. It was so much quieter at home, and I had gotten used to the street noise that came with living in the city. The fact that I slept better in noise than in the quiet made me seriously question my logic of whether or not it was healthy.

I leaned against my headboard as I listened to Michelle tell me about her sister's sorority friends and the frat parties they went to together up at Vassar. It reminded me of the fact that I had no idea what a college party was like because I hadn't been to one yet. It was also shocking to hear my best friend who was usually just as boring and thrilled by the mundane as I was, talk about having a 'wild time' at parties.

"I think he likes me. We've been texting. I'll keep you posted," she said, finally looking over at me, making me pay attention again.

"Please do." I chuckled.

"So speaking of hot guys… how are things with *Jason*?" she asked, flashing her eyebrows.

Even though Michelle and I did not get the chance to speak every day, we made sure each other was alright by religiously checking the other's social media. Jason had made a couple appearances on my stories over the past couple of months. To me, it was no big deal since he was one of the few friends I made and we lived in the same building. To Michelle, it was "the hottest tea there is." The tea was not hot, as far as I was concerned. In fact, it was cold. Iced tea, if you will.

"Alright… I told you that we're just friends." I shrugged.

"That is a load of b.s. He's so into you, and you are at least interested," she scoffed.

"So you're telling me," I deadpanned.

"No, I just know! There is a bunch of evidence. The video of you two in the pizza shop for example. He said, "wow that is the most beautiful thing I've ever seen" and you thought he was talking about the pizza, but he said, "yeah the pizza looks good, too" and then he winks! Are you crazy? *How do you not know*!" Michelle exclaimed, standing on my bed.

Her rant was interrupted when we realized Dad was standing at the door looking at her with a confused look. He cleared his throat, and she gave an apologetic smile before sitting down again.

"What's up, Dad?" I chuckled.

"We're going out for dinner soon. Michelle, you're free to join us as long as you promise to not stand on the tables and scream about us being crazy," he joked.

"I promise to not stand on tables, nor yell. I can't promise that I won't talk about your daughter being crazy." She shrugged with a comical wide-eyed look.

"Ah yes… Well, she is the craziest out of all of us." Dad winked at me from behind his glasses with a smile. I loved this man so much.

"Gee, thanks. I feel so welcomed back here." I rolled my eyes, laughing.

"That's the goal! Be down in twenty minutes," he said before he left. This time, he closed the door.

"How much of that do you think he heard?" Michelle asked.

"We'll soon know, trust me," I sighed.

We went to a fancy steakhouse we went to on special occasions. The last time I had been there was the night after my high school graduation. This time, it was a much more casual occasion. We sat in a big booth, and I found myself between Rachel and Michelle, with my parents on the other side of us. I was enjoying another heavenly bite of my mashed potatoes when I realized Mom was looking at me. It wasn't one of those looks moms give that mean nothing. It was one of those looks that made you a little nervous because you already knew there was something you haven't spoken to her about yet. I would usually try to get out of situations by acting busy, but as you can imagine, that was not really an option this time. *Here we go*, I thought.

"So Nikki, have you made a lot of friends at school yet?" Mom asked.

"Some, yeah." I smiled.

"Any boys?" she pressed.

Dad's eyes widened at that. He kept them down on his plate, but the guilt was pouring out his pores. I rolled my eyes and looked over at Michelle, who watched in amusement. Jasmine Smith never waited for what she wanted. I usually admired it, but not in times like this.

"None that are not simply friends," I said dryly.

"Um, no. There's that dreamboat Jason. If you don't get with him, I will," Rachel said with her mouth half-full.

"You will not," both Dad and I spoke at the same time.

Everyone paused for a moment. Mom looked amused, and Dad gave Rachel a look. Michelle broke the silence first with her laugh. She pushed a lock of her freshly pressed black hair behind her ear and let out the funniest sounding chuckle. If it wasn't at my expense, I would've laughed.

"I knew you liked him. I take back my crazy comment," Michelle said.

"Who's Jason?" Mom asked with an intrigued look.

"Jason is the nice gentleman that helped us with some of the boxes." Dad leaned in to quietly update her.

"Oh… *Yes, he is cute.* You two have been going on dates?" Mom asked excitedly.

"You're supposed to be on my side. She doesn't need to date," Dad said with a joking tone.

"Nicole is an adult now, Michael. She can go on dates. You want grandchildren, don't you?" she teased, making his eyebrows go up to the ceiling.

I put my hands up at that. There was no need for everyone to get the wrong idea.

"Kids? I am a kid, first of all. Second, we just hang out as friends because we are just friends." I shook my head.

"I don't know… I saw that story about the pizza and him telling you that you were the most beautiful thing he has ever seen. That sounds like a boyfriend to me," Rachel said.

I rolled my eyes and nudged her with my arm. She smiled and shrugged.

"That's what I said! Also, he's always looking her way with *the* look. I think he's into her," Michelle said.

"Can we not talk about him for thirty seconds? I am focusing on school right now. Mom, I thought you said you were so glad that I was focusing on that," I said.

"You're always focused on school. It's ok to have a social life too. Letting life gift you its surprises is ok sometimes." She shrugged.

"Ok fine, but let's drop this for now, please guys," I sighed.

That night, I tried to go to bed early to make up for the late nights studying from the past several weeks, but I just couldn't. I eventually got up and sat by my window seat. I parted the curtains and looked past the two rows of houses to look at the lake. It glistened in the moonlight. It had been so long that for once I didn't take the sight for granted.

My phone chimed, and I looked over to see my phone screen lit up in my dark bedroom. I walked over and got it. I sighed when I read the name. It was Noah.

Noah Crawford: Hey

I wondered what he wanted. It wasn't that late. I could hear Rachel laughing on the phone in the next room over. I heard the faint sound of the movie Mom and Dad watched downstairs. It wasn't even nine-thirty yet, but I had no clue what he could possibly want from me. I thought about not answering, but I did out of boredom.

Nicole Smith: What's up
Noah Crawford: How are you?
Nicole Smith: You texted me to find out how I was?

There was a pause before his next response. I could tell he was writing and then rewriting when I saw the typing bubble show up and then disappear a few times.

Noah Crawford: Yes actually, but also because *Mildred Pierce* is on. Remember when we had to watch it for class?

I remembered. We had taken a film elective together for fun after not enough people had registered for the medical one I wanted to take. We had thought it would've been fun, and it was, but it was also a lot of work. We found ourselves rewatching the movies on the weekend before the paper was due the following week.

***

"Okay, so this is way better than I thought it was going to be," I said, snuggling in closer to Noah on the couch. It was chilly, and he was like a human heater.

"I kind of wish I paid more attention in class," Noah said, pulling the blanket over my shoulders to make sure every part of me that could be warmer, was.

We had gotten to a part that was so engrossing that neither of us spoke. We didn't want to miss a word. All of a sudden, we saw Noah's mother Tracey walking through the front door.

"Hi, Mom," Noah said.

"Hi, Noah… Hi Nicole," she said, trying to sound happy about my presence but miserably failing.

She walked over to the couch and looked down from her nose at us covered in a thick blanket. It had been more for me. Noah's feet, and from the arms up, were out of the covers. He had one arm around me and one hand on the remote. She looked at me as if I was a rodent who had trespassed into her home. I wondered if I'd ever feel as if I belonged when Tracey was around.

"How are you, Ms. Crawford?" I smiled.

"Alive. I almost didn't see you there with you hiding under the covers… and my son," she said with a face that looked like she had tasted something sour.

"Someone got a little cold," Noah said, pulling me in closer, despite his mother's look.

"She could always go home if she can't handle the temperature," she sighed under her breath before she went upstairs.

***

I sighed at the memory. I looked at the moon to bring happier thoughts to my mind when I realized I never replied to Noah.

Nicole Smith: I remember! Anyway, I should get some sleep. Ttyl.

Noah Crawford: Wait. Why did you send me $6 a few days ago?

Nicole Smith: You got me lunch. I was just making sure I paid you back before I forgot.

Noah Crawford: Oh okay.

Nicole Smith: Yeah. Night.

Noah Crawford: In the future please don't do that. Cash is better.
Noah Crawford: Actually no. It's just on me.

Just when I thought guys couldn't be any more strange. I looked up at the moon this time and shook my head. She probably thought this whole thing was just as ridiculous as I did.

Nicole Smith: Okay fine.

I didn't say good night that time. I just turned my notifications off and put my phone down. The thought of how weird Noah was made me tired. I was done with the conversation.

Chapter 8

I ran on the treadmill at the school's gym and looked out at the city through the window. The only thing of noticeable color were the orange and gold treetops from the park in the distance. Everything else in the city was gray and concrete. It made me miss home. I imagined the colors of autumn surrounding the glistening lake. I thought of people having pumpkins by their doors and fallen apples garnishing the ground. It had been a month since I had been back, and I couldn't wait for Thanksgiving to come.

"What are you thinking about," Alyssa, my lab partner and faithful gym buddy, asked, breaking me out of my reverie.

"Nothing, just looking forward to visiting home soon," I answered.

"I feel that. I'm not looking forward to the long flight though," Alyssa said.

Alyssa was from Washington. Not the District of Columbia, but the state. Pretty much, she was so far that I'm fairly sure there were countries closer to New York than she was. She hadn't been home since she moved in at the end of the summer. I didn't go home every weekend, due to my heavy studying schedule, but I would go crazy if Rachel didn't show up to the apartment unannounced, or if I hadn't gone home yet for the semester. I needed my family. They were always the ones to keep me from going off the edge when things got crazy. That was why Alyssa and I became friends in the first place. I could tell how hard it was for her, and I wanted to be there. We would study and watch movies at my apartment a few times a month.

"Are we doing movies tonight?" I asked, lifting myself up and putting my feet at the side of the running belt.

"I was thinking we should switch it up," Alyssa said as her blonde ponytail bobbed around.

"Um okay... Switch it up, how?" I asked.

"Let's go to a party," she said, putting her feet to the side to stop.

I sighed. I wanted to experience a college party of course, but I just didn't want to deal with the awkwardness of trying to be social with people I didn't want to be social with. I dealt with it in high school when Michelle would drag me along. She didn't want to go much more than I did, but she would say we would regret not going one day. I'm not sure how much I agreed with that. Something told me it wouldn't be much different now.

"Um," was the only sound that could leave my lips.

"C'mon, Nicole! It'll be fun. We're young and beautiful. We can't spend this whole semester studying. We'll be together, and you can bring whoever you want, too," she pleaded.

"Maybe… I'll let you know in a few hours," I said.

"Please give me an excuse to not go to this party," I said, walking into Jason's apartment.

"Hello to you too, Smith," he said, pulling a shirt over his head.

"Oh sorry… hi," I said before doing a trust fall on his bed.

"What party?" he asked, walking over to me.

"Some party Alyssa wants to go to tonight," I said.

"You should go." He shrugged before sitting at my feet.

"No," I said, tapping his shoulder with my foot.

He broke a smile and grabbed my foot in the air. I paused because I wasn't sure what he was going to do. I had no tolerance for tickling, and unfortunately, he learned that accidentally by brushing a piece of lint off of my back. After that, I couldn't have peace. Jason's new goal was to tickle me every chance he got.

"I swear, Jason Westbrook, if you tickle me, I will destroy you," I said as I tried to pull my foot away.

"I'd like to see you try." He chuckled before taking a sneak attack on my stomach.

I shrieked while kicking and swinging my arms. I stopped once his glasses fell off his face and hit my nose.

"Ouch," I said, which made him stop.

"Sorry." He chuckled.

His phone rang and vibrated at the table next to us. He sighed before letting me go to answer it. I sat up and leaned against his headboard. He spoke while he rubbed the bridge of his nose where his glasses were. He ended the call with "thanks Mom, I love you". It made me smile, and his brown eyes shifted to me for a second before he laughed under his breath.

"So, where's the party?" he asked after putting his phone down.

"Alyssa texted me the details," I said, tossing him my phone.

"You also have a text from *my favorite person in the world*, Noah Crawford. Make sure you answer him immediately," he deadpanned, and I giggled.

I made it my job to make sure Jason and Noah would cross paths as little as possible. Our lunch incident was in the top five of the most embarrassing—as well as stressful—things I had to live through. Neither Jason nor Noah ever brought it up again, but I knew it had not been forgotten.

Jason had proven to be a super sweet guy. He was kind to everyone around me. Whenever he would see Noah that friendly smile of his would falter. I knew he didn't like him. I couldn't even blame him. Noah could have been nicer. He usually was.

"I'll just tell him I'm hanging out with my favorite, as you call yourself," I said.

"Hell yeah, I am. I'm surprised I had to help you realize it," he said, giving me an incredulous look.

"That's why I keep you around," I said sarcastically, and he laughed in response.

"Go to the party… I'll go with you. We have to get our heads out of the books at some point this semester," he said.

"Fine," I said.

I FaceTimed Alyssa as we figured out what to wear to the party. She decided on a cute red dress for herself and convinced me to put on a crop top that was really too small for me with jeans and a leather jacket.

"Are you sure? It shows a lot of cleavage and stomach," I said, looking in the mirror.

"Okay, yeah, but you are so in shape. One day, we will be like forty and saggy. Celebrate what you have now," she said, and I rolled my eyes and nodded. She had a point.

Jason met us at the address of the party. It was only a few blocks away from our building. He sat on the railing of the brownstone's steps wearing one of his untucked button-downs and dark jeans. He wasn't wearing his glasses, and I found myself missing them. He looked good regardless of what he wore, but he had the hot nerd look going on with them.

"You look… really good," Jason said with a quick once over and a small smile.

It was a simple compliment, but I realized before then Jason hadn't commented on my looks before. It kind of made my face warm up a little bit. Not that I needed a guy to tell me how good, I looked to feel good. It just made me feel even better. For a second, I forgot that I really didn't want to go to the party. Alyssa cleared her throat, and I realized she was still standing there. She was checking Jason out hard.

"This is Alyssa … Alyssa, Jason," I said introducing them both.

"Nice to meet you, Alyssa. Nicole speaks so highly of you." Jason politely shook her hand.

"Aw, well I wish Nicole told me how handsome her friend was," she said.

Jason's mouth went into a little smirk. I would be lying if I said I wasn't at least a little annoyed. How dare she make moves on a guy that I had been denying I had feelings for, for months? He was *mine*. I tried to speak to my face so I could play it off as not caring.

"Let's go in, shall we?" Jason cleared his throat.

"Ready." Alyssa giggled.

"Yup," I sighed.

There had to be almost a hundred people crammed onto the first floor of the apartment. Despite its size, it was still crowded. Jason left to get us some drinks. I wanted to mention that Alyssa in fact did not need any more to drink since I could tell she was a little more buzzed from the pregaming that I failed to take part in, but I didn't say anything.

"He is so hot," she said, grabbing my hand.

"Yeah… I guess," I said, feeling really uncomfortable.

"So you're not together or anything, right?" she asked with wide eyes.

"No… I," I began but Jason came back with our drinks.

"Here you go, ladies. I think this is jungle juice," he said, giving a slight grimace.

Jungle juice was a disgusting concoction probably made by some high school or college students who wanted to test the limits of their liver. It's usually a mixture of different alcohols and fruit punch and was never not strong. When you drink more than one cup of jungle juice, you usually have the intention of not remembering the rest of the night. I had only had it once before this party, but my little sister knew it very well. There were numerous times I would have to pick her up from parties because she was unable to make it home on her own. Long Island could be boring sometimes, and unfortunately, when a bunch of kids are stuck in a boring place, they drink.

"Lovely," I said sarcastically before taking a sip. It was quite strong, which was what I had prepared myself for.

Alyssa was on her tippy toes to get closer to Jason's ear. I rolled my eyes before looking around to see if I could recognize anyone else. What would make this situation worse would be feeling like a third wheel. I spun around and then caught someone looking right at me in the crowd. It was Noah. He had on a t-shirt that showed all his muscles and a cap on backwards. I usually hated that look, but of course, he looked good. He took a step forward and then stopped when he saw Jason. He gave me a look that said "really?" before slowly walking over.

"You came here with him?" he asked.

"Yeah and another friend," I said, not even addressing his discontent.

"What are you doing here?" he asked.

"I'm enjoying myself," I said, crossing my arms.

"You hate parties," he said knowingly.

"You don't know what I like anymore," I said, backing up from him.

Just then I felt a hand touch my arm. It was Alyssa. Her cup of jungle juice was empty. I wasn't sure how she was standing. I was pretty sure poison burned the same way as this thing.

"Jason and I are going to play spin-the-bottle starting up over by the couches," she said.

"You coming?" Jason asked with a look I couldn't read on his face.

"Sure," I said, glancing at Noah before walking over with them.

There was a huge bottle of vodka on the adjacent table with a bunch of shot glasses. I was confused about what they were for. I also wanted to know who the hell was paying for all of this when more than half of those would be broken by the end of the night.

"What are the shots for?" I asked leaning into Jason.

"Um, if you don't want to kiss the person you have to take a shot," he said in a serious tone. He looked super uncomfortable.

"You ok?" I asked.

"Yeah… you know how my stomach acts up when I'm surrounded by too many gen-z'ers," he said with a smirk.

"Oh yeah. For sure." I chuckled.

"You sure you're ok with playing? I'll sit out with you," Jason said.

"No… I'm ok. I think I'm just feeling a little of the gen-z-itis myself," I said looking over at Noah, who was still watching us.

"Alright then," Jason said with a chuckle.

The game was as dumb and petri-dish-like, as you can imagine. Guys sticking their tongues down girls that they prayed they could get more action with later and sometimes rudely declining the one they didn't think would grant them the chance. It was quite a few spins inc and it was Alyssa's turn to spin. She stood up and glanced at Jason across from her before she spun. Jason had a straight face when the top of the bottle landed in front of him. Some guys sighed in disappointment.

"Kiss or shot," a guy asked.

My stomach was in knots. Alyssa was pretty. Really pretty. She got hit on all the time. She knew how to flirt. I was sure Jason did not mind the attention he was getting from her. I looked down so I wouldn't have to watch. It was fine, I thought. I said no boys this semester anyway.

"Shot," Jason said, and some of the guys gasped.

I looked up and saw Alyssa's unhidden frown. She was surprised and so was I. The guy by the vodka handed Jason a shot, and he grimaced as he took it down. My friend sat down and finally looked over to me and raised his empty glass as if he was saying cheers. It made me smile.

The guy next to Jason chose shot when the bottle didn't fall on the girl he had been eyeing the entire game. That meant it was Jason's turn to spin. I had already been landed on by two other guys. One took a shot immediately. I wasn't sure if he didn't find me attractive or was just not interested. Either way, I was not insulted. The other tried and I took a shot. He seemed a little pissed, but I couldn't care less. I was more concerned about who Jason was going to land on. He watched the bottle intently. I was watching him watch it. Then he looked up at me. I looked down because I felt bad for staring. Then I realized it was pointed right at me. I stood up slowly. I was silent and so was Jason. We just stared at each other for what seemed like minutes.

"So… kiss or shot," the guy by the vodka asked.

Jason didn't answer and neither did I. He waited a moment and then took two steps over to me. It was like I wasn't in my body and I was a bystander. He slowly reached up to put his hand on the side of my face. He leaned, and I found myself leaning too. We were kissing. I wasn't sure how much time was passing, but I guessed a bit when I heard a guy whistle. We both pulled away at that. Jason gave me a smirk. He took a step back before I saw him almost fall to his side. I pulled myself out of my reverie and looked to see Noah yelling curse words at him.

"What the hell man," Jason said, turning to face him.

"Don't you touch her," Noah said as he looked down at him before he pushed him again.

"She's not your girl anymore. Relax," Jason said, pushing him back.

I was surprised by how much Noah moved by the push. I think he was too. I saw his fists balling at his sides. I found myself in between them within seconds. I faced Noah and could see the momentary shock on his face when I stood between them. I was far from big enough to stop a fight between Noah, who was definitely at least six feet, and Jason, who was only a few inches shorter than him.

"Nicole," Jason said sternly. He was serious whenever he said my first name.

"Nikki… get out the way," Noah said.

"No. You are not my boyfriend anymore. You can't do this Noah," I said, pointing my finger and sticking it in his chest.

Some guy that I assumed to be Noah's friend pulled him away. He looked older, but maybe he was a senior or started late. Sometimes it was hard to tell with white guys who had facial hair. The guy's back was turned to us as he tried to talk Noah down. I pulled Jason to the side and looked at the red spot on his face. He was breathing hard, and his dark eyes were piercingly cold. He was angry. Noah caught me looking at him again. I was so disappointed in him at that moment. I told him with my eyes, or at least I tried. Noah seemed to get the point when his scowl turned into an apologetic frown. *Good*, I thought. *He should be sorry.*

"I'm sorry," I said to Jason. I knew it wasn't my fault, but it was all I could think to say.

"No… it's not you… You didn't do anything," Jason said after a moment. His voice was gentle yet still harsh on the edges.

"I know, but still," I said, inspecting the spot.

"I'm kind of ready to go," he said. I agreed.

Alyssa took a cab back to her dorm building, while Jason and I walked back to our building. We were quiet for most of it. I think we were both processing everything. He insisted on walking me to my apartment. I invited him in to help ice his face. We always hung out until late at each other's places, but the vibe was different this time. He hesitated before he sat on the foot of my bed. My futon had all the night's rejected outfits on it. I sat down next to him and held the ice to his face. It looked a little bruised now. I frowned.

"It's my battle scar." He gave me a little smile.

"I'm sorry again," I said.

"You didn't do this. Don't feel like you have to fix what he's done. You may have done that in the past, but it needs to stop. Noah may think so, but the world does not owe him anything. You don't owe him anything," he said.

Chapter 9

I woke up the next morning with a stomachache. The last time I had a drink before the party was probably during the holidays, and jungle juice probably wasn't the best way to break the fast. I drank some mint tea and texted Alyssa to ask if she wanted to join me at the gym
.

Nicole Smith: I know this is not one of our scheduled days, but do you want to go to the gym?

My phone started to ring from a call from Alyssa. I accepted the call and put the phone on speaker as I looked for a gym outfit.

"Hey," I said.

"Um hi." She yawned.

"Do you want to go to the gym with me?" I asked.

"How are you not hungover," she groaned.

"I think you may have had just a little more to drink than me," I said sarcastically.

"Maybe because I wasn't busy having men fight to the death for me," she said, and I could hear the shortness in her voice.

"You might be exaggerating just a little." I rolled my eyes as I threw my clothes onto my bed.

Alyssa groaned but didn't answer. Instead, I heard the sound of running water.

"What are you doing?" I asked.

"I might go to the gym with you if I can get my life together in the next thirty minutes. I'll call you back," she said before hanging up.

Alyssa was good as new when she showed up at the gym. She had her hair in a high ponytail and was in her pink gym set. We decided to jog on the treadmill instead of the usual run due to the circumstances of the previous night. I was caught up in watching a music video on one of the TV screens when she started speaking.

"So… what happened after I left?" Alyssa asked.

"At the party? Not sure. I left at the same time you did," I said.

"With Jason?" she asked suggestively.

"Um… yeah," I answered as I glanced over at her.

Alyssa made a weird noise under her breath. It made me chuckle, and I almost missed my step. I pushed myself up, put my feet on the side of the running belt, and looked at her. I decided it was time for a water break.

"So… you're hooking up with him," she said, more than asking, and that made me sputter water on my shirt.

"What?" I coughed as I tried to clear my windpipe.

She gave me a knowing look before she hopped off the treadmill. I followed, still trying to clear the water that insisted on being in my lungs.

"Nicole, if I knew that something was going on between you two, I would've never tried to make a move on your boy toy," she said, walking over to the lockers.

"No. No, no, no, and no. Boy toy? We are not," I continued, coughing in between my words.

"You don't have to lie to me." She finally turned around and tapped my back.

I finally got the water out and took a few breaths. I tightened the cap on my bottle. Water would have to come after I finished having this conversation.

"Alyssa, I am not doing anything with Jason. I'm not even sure what's going on," I said.

"So… something is going on with that other guy? Who is he, anyway? He's drop-dead gorgeous too! Please tell me where you're meeting these perfect men," she said as we grabbed our stuff from our lockers.

"Oh… Noah. He's my ex and definitely not perfect," I said.

Alyssa came out from behind her locker with raised eyebrows. I rolled my eyes and led the way out of the gym.

"I didn't know you were dating someone before," she said in a loud, scandalized way.

"We dated before I knew you," I said.

"Was it long-term?"

"Yeah. Over a year."

"So you two decided to go to the same school before the breakup? That's a really bold choice."

"We broke up two years ago," I deadpanned.

"And he's acting like a maniac? Wow, I don't know if that's love or just crazy," she gasped and made the group of girls walking by in the hall look at us like we were crazy.

I put my hand on her freckled shoulder and put my finger over my lips. I would prefer the world not know about my farce of a love life.

"Definitely crazy," I finally answered.

"I *love* a good love triangle." She gave a little golf clap.

"It's stressful," I sighed before opening the door that led outside.

"Keep me posted. See you later," she said before she went along her way.

Jason and I had tests we had to study for, so the next day, he brought Chinese food over to my apartment and we got to work immediately. I was in the process of making online flashcards, and Jason was highlighting away in his book when we heard a knock on the door. Jason raised his glasses to the top of his head and walked over to the door. I could see his body tense the moment he opened it.

"What are you doing here," Noah's voice asked.

"I was invited, unlike you," Jason snapped back, and for a moment, I was shocked by his tone of voice.

I slowly stood up to catch Noah's jaw already tightening. Not again. He was the last person I wanted to see right now. Anyone would've been better. I would've welcomed Reggie's ghost more than Noah at that moment. Okay, that was morbid, but you get what I mean.

"Where is she?" Noah finally asked after a deep, audible exhale.

"I'm right here… but why are you?" I finally asked, walking to the door.

Jason stepped aside, but still stood there. He looked furious. Despite what he had told me about being over the almost fight, I knew he wasn't. This was my proof. I had two different forms of male ego radiating in my apartment. One thought he was smarter than the other, and one thought he was stronger than the other. I'll keep my opinions as to how accurate they were to myself.

"I was going to ask if you wanted to hang out or something… give me a chance to explain myself, but I guess you have company," Noah finally said.

"Yeah… sorry," I said.

"What are you doing anyway?" he asked.

"None of your business," Jason muttered.

Noah put his eyebrow up at that and smirked at me as if to ask if I could hear how ridiculous this was. I sighed because it was ridiculous. They *both* were getting on my nerves. I knew what was coming wasn't good. Noah was usually a complete sweetheart, but once someone eyed what he thought was his, he was a completely different person. I was not his anymore, but I had a feeling Noah had forgotten that.

"Right… because there's so much business here for me to mind. Nikki, you should go back to your little study party," Noah mocked.

"You wouldn't know about that, would you," Jason said.

"And what's that supposed to mean?" Noah asked.

Jason just chuckled and shrugged his shoulders before walking back to his seat. Noah's eyes followed him for a moment before looking at me. He was looking for answers in my eyes. I could tell. What I couldn't figure out was what exactly was he trying to ask me. After a long moment of silence, he asked me if we could go out a few hours the next day for brunch, and it was his treat. I made up an excuse. I just didn't want to speak to him after what happened. When I turned back, I could see Jason's pained expression.

"What?" I asked, sitting back down on my bed.

"Nothing," he said as he moved around on the futon.

"You're so full of it," I said, throwing a pillow at him.

Jason just stared back at me for a moment. I froze and just looked back. I thought I had insulted him.

"Sorry," I said, unsure of what was going on with him.

"It's not that. I just… can we talk," he said.

My scalp started to prickle. I was sure he was going to bring up the previous night. We couldn't not talk about it. I needed clarity on it even if he didn't.

"I decided to look into the Crawford case again," Jason said with his hands folded in his lap.

My body was frozen. I wasn't sure if I was going to deck him in the face or cry. I did neither. Both would've been a better choice.

"Are you insane?" I asked.

"What? No. Listen, Nicole, I know you have a soft spot for Noah, but he's hiding something. I can tell. I could be wrong of course, but if he is, he deserves to be in jail. I don't care who he is." Jason stood up.

"Jason, that whole case brought hell to everyone around him. *That includes me*. I went through so much pain." I stood up to face him.

"I'm not going to bring you into this. You don't have to be questioned. The press is not going to be at your door like they were two years ago. I will keep you out of this. I promise," he said softly as he took a step forward and put his hands on my shoulders.

"Whatever. If I can't stop you then… just whatever," I said as I pulled away from him and went back to sit down.

"I know you're mad, but I promise I will always have your back. Everything will be ok," he said.

Waking up in my bed at home instead of my bed at the apartment was weird no matter how many times I had done it at this point. I had gotten so used to my apartment that now being at the house felt foreign to me. It was way more comfortable though, and my body appreciated it. I made a mental note to get another mattress pad for the apartment.

I rolled over to look at my phone to find five missed calls from Noah. I sat up at the sight. I pressed on his name and called him back.

"We need to talk," Noah answered immediately in a hushed tone.

"What? No Happy Thanksgiving Eve," I deadpanned in a sleepy voice.

Noah gave a deep sigh that made me chuckle just a little. He was so dramatic sometimes, and I figured this was one of those times. I think pretty boys always had some type of complex. Noah's was that when something went wrong, he would act like the world was ending.

"You need to tell your boyfriend to knock it off," he said after a moment of silence.

I rolled my eyes so hard that I was surprised it wasn't audible. I looked at the clock and it read 10:35 am. This boy was calling me at this early hour because of a guy that was not my boyfriend. I had no clue what was going on, but I had so many other things to worry about. *I really should consider the convent*, I thought.

"I don't have a boyfriend," I sighed.

"You know who I'm talking about. That Jacob kid," he bit back.

"Jesus, Noah. His name is Jason. You literally decked him in the face, and you don't know his name? What about him? What has he done that is so bad that you had to call me a ridiculous amount of times in a row?" I asked.

Noah was silent for a moment. Then I heard some shifting from the other end of the line. He was moving around. Then I heard the sound of a door close. I wondered who he was with. Then I reminded myself that I was not supposed to care.

"He is snooping around with stuff that we buried a couple years ago… if you catch what I mean," he said.

I did. I paused for a moment and thought about how dangerous this game Jason was playing. Then I remembered how much he didn't like Noah and how he felt like he had nothing to lose, emphasis on *felt*. Something told me that was not the actual reality.

"I don't think he's snooping around in anything," I tried to play it off, but I knew he probably was.

"My neighbor in the dorms saw him on campus today, and he was asking him way too much about my life before college. Then he asked about my family and why we moved. He didn't know, but imagine he did," Noah said, and I could hear the irritation in his voice.

"So, you're telling me this because?" I asked.

"Tell him if he doesn't stop, he's going to run into some serious problems. I'm not kidding around. If you don't take care of him, I will," Noah said.

Chapter 10

I was home, but my mind was back on campus and what obstacles waited for me when I got back. I had to pass my finals, as well as figure out what to do with Jason. My mind was running a mile a minute, and I hadn't even realized that Dad was trying to talk to me from across the table. Rachel reached over and pinched my arm.

"Ouch! Why?" I asked and looked over at her.

"Dad's been trying to speak to you for a decade. Come back to Earth." She shook her head before putting another scoop of stuffing on her plate.

"Sorry Dad," I sighed before taking a mouthful of cranberry sauce.

Dad just stared at me for a moment. His face was placid, but his eyes had a tinge of concern. He was starting to notice that something was wrong. That was unacceptable. I used to zone out a lot when things went wrong two years before. I started having panic attacks. Then, I started therapy. My parents blamed it on the stress of the case and my breakup with Noah. They weren't wrong. That was part of it, but I knew where all the stress had specifically come from.

"I was just asking when your last final is." He raised an eyebrow.

"Honey, you've been quiet all day. Is it a class that's bothering you?" Mom asked before I could answer him.

If I could personally thank God himself for giving me that out, I would. I nodded yes and sighed as if I had been caught. I would have to poorly act my way out of this one.

"Yeah, you know my biology class is really getting intense. I don't want to start off my first semester of college with a less than good enough GPA," I said.

My leg bobbed under the table. I hated lying, and every time I did, I felt like my insides were going to explode… or melt… maybe both. Either way, I felt sick every time I did.

"I'm sure you're doing fine, Coco. Whenever I call, you're either studying, eating, or working out," Rachel said.

"Well, the working out is recent. I don't want to gain the freshman fifteen. I want to still look good." I shrugged as I tried to seem nonchalant.

I saw Rachel look over at Mom and flash her eyebrows. Mom snickered before taking a bite of mac and cheese. I rolled my eyes and looked over at Dad, who clearly was confused by all these silent exchanges. Men.

"What? I don't get it," Dad finally said, making Mom laugh audibly this time.

"You're always laughing at me," Dad said with a fake pout. Mom kissed him on the cheek in response.

"Look good for who? Jason?" Rachel laughed.

"My own self." I shook my head.

"Enough! Not at the dinner table," Dad shook his head as if he was trying to shake the thoughts out of his head.

After dinner and a few board games, I went upstairs. I was talked-out, and I needed some time to myself. My social battery could only go on for so long, even with family. I got in bed and started to read a book that I had been taking too long to read. Then I heard my door open and close. I looked up to see Rachel in her pajamas and bonnet. She was ready for bed.

"Okay, so what are you lying about?" Rachel said.

I sat up and looked at her quizzically. A girl couldn't even read in her bed in peace. I had no idea what she was talking about, so I just blinked.

"You know… the biology class thing. That's not what's bothering you. It's something else," she said before jumping onto the foot of my bed.

"It is about biology," I lied.

"You told me a couple weeks ago that you got the highest grade in the class," Rachel scoffed.

"Well… I didn't do as well on the next test. I just have to work on it. It's fine. We don't have to talk about this," I rambled.

She had that look that meant she was suspicious. I knew what the look meant because we had almost the same face, and I would usually be the one using it with her. I walked over to the bathroom to wash my face for the night. It was the perfect way for me to hide my expressions.

"Something is wrong, and you might as well tell me now because I will find out whatever it is," she said.

I didn't answer. I just rolled my eyes as I rubbed my face with a makeup wipe. The last thing I wanted to do was get Rachel involved in all of this. *She doesn't deserve to have the burden of it all*, I thought.

"I'm not leaving until you tell me something. You always hold things in. You're going to explode one day," she huffed, crossing her arms.

"It's just boy stuff... I need time to process before we talk about it, Rach," I lied while rubbing my face with soap to cover my expression.

Rachel was silent for a moment. I could tell she was trying to figure out if I was telling the truth or not. My stomach hurt a little at the thought of lying to her. I never liked lying to her, and I hardly ever did. The last time I could remember was around the time of the incident.

***

The doorbell rang, and I felt even sicker than I did before. My skin felt prickly and hot, as if I was moments away from fainting. I tried to take one of those deep, silent breaths that would help a little, but not as much as the audible ones.

Dad opened the door and two detectives walked in. They had that fake smile on their faces that was more for professionalism and not to actually be nice. Mom used that smile whenever someone she couldn't yell at upset her. I don't remember what they said, but I knew they were here to ask me questions about Noah. It had been over three weeks since the incident, and he was now a suspect. The thought of him being locked away consumed me and kept me up most nights.

I had practiced this day in my head multiple times. I would play the role that everyone expected me to play. People seemed to ask the least questions about what they thought they knew. I played innocent and naive. I wasn't, but I even had my parents fooled and I lived with them.

"So, Miss Smith, did Noah Crawford ever say anything out of the ordinary about his uncle, Reginald Crawford?" the woman asked.

"Hmm… I think Noah said that he won a pie eating contest once when he was in the seventh grade… that's pretty weird. I could never eat that much." I laughed.

The two inspectors gave me that smile that people give to someone who they think is severely dumb or young, *or both*. They chuckled and looked at my Dad with a smile.

"So… has Noah ever expressed being upset with his uncle? Did he dislike him?" the man asked.

"Noah really never hated anyone. He's so nice and calm. I think he would only get upset about video games sometimes. If anything, I think he would be happy to help his uncle." I nodded with a smile.

"And you two date, right? Has he mentioned anything to you about this?" the woman asked.

"Yes, he's my boyfriend, and nope. He just said that he hopes he shows up soon. I get worried easily, so he probably didn't want me to worry and didn't say more," I said.

"Did Noah kill Reginald? We have reason to believe he might have," the woman pressed.

My heart was beating so fast. I was sure that at any moment I would faint. I was so stressed that I wanted to cry. I tilted my head to the side and gave a horrified look.

"My little Noey wouldn't hurt anyone," I said.

"So, for the record, you're saying you don't know anything of Noah Crawford having anything to do with Reginald Crawford's disappearance?" the man asked.

"Nope. I have no idea where Reggie could be," I said.

"What were you doing the day of July 10th?" the woman asked.

"Hmm, I think I rode my bike and had some ice cream with friends later that afternoon," I said.

"You think or you know?" the woman asked.

"I know," I said.

"Was Noah there?" the man asked.

"Yeah. He met us over there," I said.

When they left, Rachel sat next to me on the couch. She leaned on my shoulder and hugged me.

"You ok?" she asked.

"Yeah, I just hate this whole thing," I said.

"You don't know anything about Noah, right?" she whispered.

I pulled away and looked at her. She looked me in the eyes with a frown. My stomach started to turn.

"Why would you ask me that?" I asked.

"Because you hold your breath when you lie. You do it so you don't fidget… and you hardly breathed during that whole thing," she said, looking down.

"I'm just scared of those detectives. I don't like being questioned." I shook my head.

"Okay," Rachel said quietly.

***

The day I got back to campus, I unpacked the new winter clothes I brought from home. It was not warm anymore. The light jackets gave way to the heavier ones. I needed gloves and heavy boots. Things were changing outside, just like the vibe of the semester. Everyone was cracking down from due dates and finals that were around the corner. I took the time to mark my calendar and organize what needed to be done for the next few weeks. I used my different colored pens and color-coded everything the way I liked it.

I was just about done when I heard a knock on my door. I assumed it was Jason. He had texted me earlier that day and I didn't answer. I just needed some me-time. I threw on a pair of shorts underneath the large t-shirt I was wearing around my hot apartment. I opened the door to see Noah. His clothes were wet from the rain. His eyes were intense… again. I started to wonder if his face was just stuck like that.

"You weren't answering your phone," he said when I narrowed my eyes at his presence.

"I have things to do. Is that all?" I asked.

"No, we have to talk. This is life or death," he answered.

Chapter 11

Ideally, I would have closed the door in Noah's face and not given the situation a second thought. There wasn't a single part of me that wanted to speak to him, but when you have a secret with someone like the one we did, there are some things that you have no power over. After a needed cup of tea, a towel, and the only oversized hoodie that I could lend to Noah awkwardly being one from the high school he had to leave, we spoke.

"Jason's father is a cop," Noah said.

"Okay, so let's define what life or death information is," I deadpanned.

"He was able to get access to some files from the original investigation. Cops know other cops," Noah said.

"How did you find that out?" I asked.

"Don't worry about that. What you need to worry about is getting that little dick to drop this," Noah said.

I looked up at the ceiling in response to the jab. It was annoying, but I was nowhere near surprised. I also looked up there for any extra patience that could be salvaged, but there was none to be found.

"First of all, don't talk to me like that. I'm not one of your friends. Second, I tried. He's not budging especially after what you did last weekend. That was dumb." I crossed my arms.

"Fine, I'm sorry. I shouldn't speak to you like that. However, I would love to find out what we are if it's not friends," Noah said as he flashed his eyebrows.

"A contact," I said as I sassily looked at him from over my shoulder and walked to the kitchen to refill my mug with hot water.

"*A contact*," he scoffed.

"Yeah." I shrugged with a smirk that I couldn't hold in from the little bit of triumph I felt.

Noah gave me a smirk of his own. His look was way too familiar and all of a sudden, I felt so vulnerable. We both stared at each other for a moment, and everything became so uncomfortable. I was sure he felt it too once he looked down and cleared his throat. When he looked up, it was all a thing of the past. His expression was all back to business again.

"Anyway, what I was going to say is if Jason's upset about what happened to him at the party, then he's going to be even more upset about what happens if he doesn't stop pushing this case," Noah said with an exasperated expression.

"Okay, relax. I'll figure it out. Killing one person is enough. I don't think you need another," I said without thinking.

Noah froze and turned to fully face me slowly. There was hurt in his eyes, and his jaw was tense. I had been annoyed with him, but I immediately felt sorry. That was something I shouldn't have used against him. I knew I would die, for lack of a better term, if someone ever did the same to me. Not that I would ever kill someone.

"I told you already that it wasn't me," he said.

"Noah, I'm sorry for saying that. That was low, but you expect me to just believe that? That's crazy. I saw you. You told me you did," I said, rubbing my temples.

"You saw nothing. You saw the aftermath, and I told you a story. It was safer that way," he said.

I sighed and started to pace. This was not how I thought my weekend was going to go.

"I need you to stop him. You have to find a way," Noah said as he walked to the door.

"Fine. I'll try again," I said, giving him the answer he wanted to hear.

He stopped before he opened the door and looked at me. His eyes softened a little bit. He was looking at my hair before smiling at me.

"Did you cornrow your hair yourself?" he asked.

"Yeah." I shrugged.

"It looks nice." He smiled before he walked out and closed the door behind him.

I walked over to the bathroom mirror and looked at my eight cornrows going down to the back of my head. I was confused about why he brought it up, and then I remembered.

***

"How does it feel? Am I hurting you?" Noah asked with a chuckle.

"No. I just want to see," I said, pausing the video on my laptop.

Noah had seen me braiding my hair once before and asked if he could learn. He thought it was fascinating. At first, I told him that there was no way I was going to let him braid my hair. I loved Noah, but I wasn't sure what would happen if I let a white guy handle my brilliantly uncontrollable hair. I knew he had no experience with hair that was coarser than his slightly wavy hair. After a couple months, I finally relented and let him try braiding on my head instead of the old mannequin head I had in my room. He genuinely wanted to learn, and I thought it was sweet.

"Alright! I did one," he said before handing me a hand mirror.

I looked and saw a rather neat cornrow going down my scalp. I tilted the mirror and saw a proud Noah smiling at his work. I put the mirror down and turned to him. He frowned and rubbed his probably sore fingers.

"Do you like it? Why are you turning around? I have like three more to do," he said.

"You want to do the rest?" I asked with a chuckle.

"I have to keep practicing. One day, I'll have to help you do this stuff on smaller heads," he said softly.

I grabbed his face and kissed him. He kissed me back, and for moments, we lost track of everything around us. Time and its origin did not matter for he was the only thing I was trying to keep track of. His hands started to slide down to my waist as he leaned in more until we heard a knock on my door. We both opened our eyes to see Rachel standing there. She had her arms crossed with a smirk on her face.

"Ooo…," she said.

Noah smiled. I rolled my eyes as he let me go after giving me one more kiss on my cheek.

"Yes Rach?" I asked.

"Noah, Mom wants to know if you are coming to Thanksgiving dinner next week… but I'm going to assume you are," she said, wagging her eyebrows.

"Yes Rachel, I'll be there." He laughed.

I think we both assumed she would leave, but Rachel walked in and looked at my hair. Then she looked at my computer screen that had a paused braiding tutorial on it. She smirked.

"Are you learning how to braid?" she asked, looking at Noah.

"Yeah. I've been practicing. Look at the one I did." He smiled proudly.

Rachel walked around to the back of me and ran a finger across it. When she came back into my view, she had a look of approval on her face. That meant she was *definitely* impressed.

"You did good. *I'm impressed.* Anyway, I have to go to dance practice. Mom said to behave while she's out the house, you two," she said before she sauntered out the room.

"I feel so validated." Noah smiled, and it reached his eyes.

I always liked it when he smiled like that.

***

The next morning, I made breakfast and brought it in Tupperware bowls down to Jason. If there was anything he loved, it was breakfast. If there was one way to get Jason Westbrook to do something you wanted, it was bring him food. I knew the combination would guarantee positive results. I brought down french toast, bacon, and eggs and knocked on his door. There was no answer. He was a heavy sleeper. I put the bowl down by the door and looked around to see if anyone else was around before I pulled up the little piece of carpet at a corner where he left his spare key. I opened the door to see him sleeping shirtless with his earbuds in. I tried my best not to stare for more than ten seconds. I failed.

I pressed pause on his phone's screen and gently pulled the buds out. He didn't move at all. I sighed and opened up his blinds to let more light in. I was about to call his name when I looked at his little bulletin of pictures on the wall. There were pictures from Jason's debate team competitions, the DC trip he went on with the United Democratic League, his family, but there were so many with me in them. There was one of us at the freshman mixer, one of us at his first debate, one of me giving him the finger while peeking out from behind his fridge and one of us sitting down doing work in the park. I stopped to remember the memories of each day.

That's when the thing that I had been trying to suppress came front and center in my mind. What was going on between us? There was no reason for me to doubt that he had feelings for me. I knew that. I had known that for months. What I was worried about was whether he would want me despite what I had done and all the mess that came because of it. He was the do-good type of guy and I was that type of girl, *except* for the one thing that kept me from completely doing that.

"You're a terrible criminal, Smith. You break in to look at my embarrassing collection of semester pics," Jason's voice said from behind me.

I jumped and turned around. I gave him an annoyed look and pushed him before I realized he was still shirtless. Jason didn't have on his glasses, but I'm sure he didn't need them to notice me looking. It should be illegal to look that good first thing in the morning.

"Is that food?" Jason asked, walking over to his little table.

"Yeah, I made breakfast," I said, watching his back muscles move as he stretched. I had to get a grip.

"I'll wash up. You can start eating. Does this mean I have to cook when we hang out? This is so nice, but I don't know how to boil an egg." He flashed me a smile before he went into the bathroom.

"How do you sustain life, Westbrook?" I asked as I got plates.

"With a very empty wallet and nice meal plan," Jason called from the bathroom.

"You toned up... Someone's been working out," I stammered and immediately regretted saying it.

I palmed my forehead and wondered for a moment how I ever got to get a guy to like me in the past with the inability to ever sound smooth. The water in the bathroom turned off, and Jason walked out with a smirk on his face. He sat at the table with just his sweatpants.

"Yeah, I figured I would start working out. Why not? You think I look good?" he asked smugly.

"Yeah," I said, grabbing a couple pieces of bacon for my plate.

"Well, what a coincidence. I think you're quite aesthetically pleasing yourself," he said, purposely getting close to get the french toast.

I smiled but was too shy to look at him. I didn't even think of flirting. I was too much of a dork for that. I had accepted it. There were already too many people trying to be cool in the world. Whatever *cool* meant anyway. We ate in silence for a while until Jason asked what made me get up so early on a Sunday. I shrugged and said that I was usually up by nine anyway, but usually stayed in bed for a little.

"What are your plans for the day?" I asked.

"Just study for my quiz and then finish reading some of the… stuff," he hesitated at the end.

"The documents for the case," I finished for him because there was no sense in pretending that's not what he meant.

"I didn't want to… you know," he hesitated.

"It's okay. Have you found anything new?" I asked, trying to sound as nonchalant as possible.

"Nothing yet. I can let you know when I do if you want. I might have a few questions…," he said, walking over to his bedside table to grab his glasses and laptop.

I thought about the offer for a moment. *This might be my way to keep an eye on things*, I thought. I nodded in response, and he smiled. He read some more on his laptop next to me at the table, and I looked at my phone like the awkward girl that I am. I looked up to just glance at him and found him looking at me.

"Actually, I'm glad you're here. I wanted to talk to you about the elephant in the room," he said, closing the screen halfway.

I knew this was the conversation that I had been trying to avoid for the past week. I got super nervous and started to play with my thumbs.

"I know I ate a lot this past vacation, but please be easy on me, Westbrook," I joked to ease my nerves, but caused Jason to snicker in response.

"No, you look amazing. What I mean is last week at the party when I… I kissed you," he said, staring hard at the table and not at my face.

"Yeah… that," I said underneath my breath.

He finally looked at me through his long eyelashes with a face I could not read. *Was I supposed to say something*, I wondered. I looked around while I tried to find words.

"I was wondering… Okay, so I'm not good at being romantic. I've only had like one girlfriend, and that was like two years ago. We dated for a couple weeks. I just don't know what I'm doing here. I just know that I'm kind of into you. No, correction, I'm very much into you. I just don't know how you feel. You're one of the only people our age that I like being around. I like us like this, and I want us to be friends, but also more… Smith, please say something," he rambled, and for the first time, Jason did not have a joke or sarcastic comment to end something that was mildly serious.

I didn't know what to say. I was shocked, and it left me speechless. It wasn't that I was choosing not to speak, but words couldn't come out due to my shock. Jason's were sweet enough. I didn't need poems or flowers… I found so much comfort in his openness; his uncomplicated-ness.

"I don't… I don't know what to say," I said in a whisper, and I'm pretty sure a ridiculous smile formed on my face. Whatever my face was saying made Jason's bare shoulders relax.

"There isn't a right or wrong thing to say. I just want to know what you're thinking," he said, running his hand through his curls.

"I'm thinking a lot and maybe that's the problem. I wonder if this will ruin our friendship. I'm wondering if we've given this enough time. I'm wondering... nothing." I stopped myself before I said the main thing that was keeping me back.

Jason reached over, and, at first, I thought he was going to kiss me again. I held my breath involuntarily at the thought and wanted to cringe at the butterflies I felt in my stomach. He was close to my face but just stayed there. He hesitated before he took one of my hands. He played with my fingers similarly to how I was fumbling with them in my lap.

"You know you can talk to me, right," he said softly.

"Yeah, I know. It's just complicated," I whispered back.

"We don't have to make it complicated... Do you like me back?" he asked.

"Yeah," I said.

"Cool... so what makes you sound so unsure?" he asked.

"I'm not sure I'm what you want or vice versa honestly," I sighed.

"Well, I don't know either... I think it's worth exploring though." He gave me a small smile.

I wondered if he would feel the same way if this all came to light. The thought made my mind race.

Chapter 12

So, I didn't really have a boyfriend, but I really didn't *not* have one either. It was a weird concept that I was not willing to explain to anyone. When Michelle called that afternoon, I left that particular update out because I knew I would get no studying done if I told her I was in anything that resembled a relationship. Even if I did, I wouldn't have known what to tell her. Jason and I were just testing the waters.

"I miss you! You sound like your mind is elsewhere. How are you doing?" Michelle asked for the second time during the conversation.

"I told you I was fine," I sighed.

"Whatever. I'm going to let this slide because I know you're studying, but when you come back home, I'll find out."

It had been days since I had even thought about my original intentions of going to see Jason that morning. I hadn't thought about it until later that week when I was sitting in the cafeteria later at night than usual. It was raining heavily, and of course, it was my luck that I forgot my umbrella. Alyssa was next door at the gym and promised to walk me to my building door on the way to her dorm. Jason was in Brooklyn for a debate.

I had been staring at my laptop for hours, going over the five hundred terms I needed to know for my final, when I felt someone's presence over my shoulder. I turned around to see Noah standing there.

"So, you're just going to stand there and watch me?" I asked.

"I just got here. I wasn't sure if it was you," he said, walking around to sit at the chair in front of me.

"What can I do for you, Noah?" I asked, leaning back and rubbing my tired eyes.

"So, did you speak to him?" he asked.

"What?" I asked, moving my fingers from my eyes to look at him.

"Jason. Did you speak to him about the stuff?" he asked, scanning the room before looking at me again.

I immediately felt stressed when I realized I hadn't mentioned it to Jason. This was exactly why I did not want to get involved with a boy during my first semester of college. I could've been studying, but, because I forgot to get my kind-of-boyfriend to drop a murder case that I was a complete accomplice of, I had to take a break. Like I said, having a boyfriend was *definitely* the main problem here. I was distracted and what I forgot to do literally had to do with Jason—the guy who was, in fact, distracting me.

"Yeah," I said, opening back up my laptop to partially hide myself from Noah.

"Okay, and what did he say?" he asked after a small suspicious pause. Crap.

"He said he found another case that caught his eye." I shrugged with a chuckle.

Noah seemed to ease his posture a little bit. *I actually fooled him*, I thought. He laughed at the idea and sat back in his chair.

"The kid's crazy, but whatever. Now I don't have to deal with… everything," he said, and it sounded so ominous that I looked up.

"What do you mean by everything? We don't know if he was going to find anything anyway," I said.

"Yeah, but it's not just me he would have issues with. It's a lot of shit he would be in. That's what I was trying to warn you about. Anyway, if you're saying he's dropping it, then we're all good," he said, standing up.

Noah bid me farewell and left the cafeteria. He seemed to be at ease, but I was the opposite. Was Noah just bluffing, or was there some serious trouble on the horizon for Jason? Something told me Jason had no clue what kind of trouble he could be facing. I couldn't even warn him, especially when I had no idea what kind of trouble it was. I had to think of something to fix this, and I had to find out before Jason.

Classes had ended for the fall semester and finals started in a couple days. If you weren't crying, procrastinating, or contemplating dropping out, you were studying. I didn't have the chance to enjoy not having class because I went to every review session that my professors offered. I might've been a little burnt out, which was bad, but the way I saw it, that A would always be there. I could recover from the burnout.

My curls were pulled back in a scrunchy that was on the verge of popping. I ran down the block in my sweats and fleece jacket. I lost track of time looking over terms and was five minutes from being late to the last Bio 101 review. I waited for the light to change so I could cross when I felt eyes on my back. For a second, I thought it was Noah, but then when I turned around, he wasn't there. I didn't see anyone I knew.

I got distracted by a young couple holding hands as they walked by. They looked so happy, and I frowned. I wasn't jealous. I loved seeing happy couples. It just reminded me of the fact that my love life was a complete and utter mess. I had an ex who may or may have not been a killer, and a current guy who I worried about getting too close to because of my ex. I grimaced to myself.

I looked back to the couple, whose backs were all I could see at that point. The girl had a jacket that said, "stay young and free". I couldn't help but think about someone else who had a similar motto.

***

Noah's hand found mine silently and intertwined its fingers with mine. I turned to him and kissed his cheek. He was turned to the window, looking at the moon through the thin curtains.

"What's wrong?" I asked, laying on his chest.

"Nothing… why?" he asked, squeezing my hand.

"You're so quiet," I said.

"I'm just enjoying the moment. I'm here with you and the moon is almost as beautiful as you," he said. I could almost hear his smirk that he always had when he complimented me.

"I like that about you," I said.

"What's that?" he asked.

"You are always so relaxed. I'm always not. Not even now," I sighed.

"You're stressed? Even now?" Noah chuckled, patting my butt from over the covers.

"I'm thinking about studying for the SATs and college and …," I began.

Noah made a shushing sound and kissed my forehead. I stopped talking and just sighed.

"Listen, Nikki… we are living our last few years as kids. Let's just be kids. Yes, all of that is important, but let's just live in the now for a moment," he said softly.

"It's hard. There's so much to do… we're growing up." I smiled because I was next to him, but still sighed.

"Don't let growing up kill the precious parts of you that should never die," he said.

"The precious parts?" I asked.

He turned around and looked at me. His eyes were happy but tired. Something told me that mine looked the same.

"The parts of you that you got from being a kid… Y'know like asking questions and being open-minded. Having fun. Being able to… to relish in the warmth of the present. Don't become old and unable to accept things that are different. We should still want to have fun and not let life make us bitter or unhappy, like some of our parents and grandparents," he said.

I didn't answer. Instead, I just thought about it. *He was right,* I thought. I wouldn't let the stresses of life change the parts of me that I liked; the innate parts of me that were untouched by the abrasive reality of growing up.

Everything was so calm that night and that summer… until it all went downhill exactly one week later.

***

The light changed, and I crossed the street. I didn't have time to look around more, but every chance I got, I looked over my shoulder. Since everything had happened, I tried my best to work on my paranoia. Before I left home, Rachel and I even worked on me not reaching for my bat every time I heard a noise at night. Over time, I had become a lot calmer, but I had a weird feeling in my stomach. I felt like I was being followed. I stopped again and turned around, just to catch someone hiding behind a corner. Part of me wanted to check who it was, but the other part—the smarter part—convinced me otherwise. Something told me that if I did, I would be in more danger than I was already in at that very moment. I ran the next few blocks to the building the review was in and then pulled out my phone. My original thought was to text Jason, but then I wondered if Noah would be better to contact in a situation like this one.

Nicole Smith: Hi. Can you meet me at the location I'm sending you at 3?
Noah Crawford: I can… Is everything ok?
Nicole Smith: Not sure.
Noah Crawford: Ok. See you at 3.

I grabbed a cup of tea and met Noah by the entrance of the science building. He was standing right inside the doors, rubbing his hands together from the cold. His expression was full of concern.

"Are you ok?" he asked before I could say a word.

"I might be crazy, but I think I was being followed on my way here," I said.

Noah was silent for a moment. He didn't move except for his eyes. They narrowed.

"Did you see who it was?" he asked.

"A guy… kind of tall. He had on a beanie. I think he was blonde, but like I said, he had on a beanie so…," I said, scanning my memory.

He was silent again, and something about his lack of questions or real concern made me think he already had a lot of the answers. I adjusted the bag on my shoulder before I crossed my arms.

"Do you know anything about this?" I asked.

Once again, he did not answer. Instead, he looked past me as he thought. I wasn't sure how to react. I was too scared to be angry, even though I was quite peeved about the whole thing.

"I'm not sure what's going on, but for now I'm going to walk you home," he said, reaching for my arm.

"You're lying," I said, taking a step back.

Noah looked really uneasy. He didn't look mad. He didn't look annoyed. He looked uncomfortable and a little scared, which did not help my nerves.

"I don't know what's happening… yet. If it's what I think it could be, then we might need to worry. Until I find out, I need you to stay in your apartment," he said, getting close and lowering his voice.

"I have a final tomorrow," I said.

"Fine. Don't go anywhere else," he said, nodding his head in the direction of the door.

I followed and walked closely next to him. The air was cold, and I wished I had worn a coat instead of my fleece. I took a sip of my tea. The sky had turned very dark and overcast. I couldn't blame her. I felt that way too. When we got to the corner where I saw the guy, I mentioned it. Noah stared at it for a moment before we crossed the street.

"Do you have something to do with this?" I asked, not knowing why I felt the need to.

"I… I might," he said, looking straight ahead and not at me.

"You're really ridiculous, you know that." I stopped and glared at him.

Noah stopped a few steps ahead of me and groaned. People glanced at us before making their way around us. That was the beautiful curse of New York City. There were people everywhere—so many that we took each other for granted. We didn't stop or even care what the other was doing. We all had things to do and places to be. It was lonely, but you did, in fact, get a healthy dose of privacy because of it. Unless you were me, of course.

"I didn't do this, but I might know who did. Just relax, ok," he said.

"Relax when I'm in danger?" I gave him an incredulous look.

"You're not in danger," Noah said, but he sounded completely unsure.

Noah insisted on walking me to my apartment door, and after realizing I had no choice in the matter, I let it happen. We walked into my building to see Jason waiting for the elevator. He had a smile when he first saw me, but then it faltered just a bit when he saw Noah walk in behind me.

"He lives here," Noah grumbled.

"Yeah," I said.

He huffed out a loud breath and crossed his arms.

"Hi," Jason said.

"Hey… You finished your paper?" I asked awkwardly.

"I did. I was actually going to chill with you while I got started on the next one. Noah, how are you?" he asked, trying to sound as friendly as possible as all three of us walked into the elevator.

"I'm good. There was an armed robbery in the area, and I told Nicole I would drop her home," Noah said, leading me in with a hand on my shoulder.

"Oh well… that was nice of you." Jason nodded with his eye on Noah's hand.

I expected Noah to say something suggestive about always being nice to me. I knew how he operated. He didn't though. Instead, he gave a small smile and nodded. The elevator opened to my floor, and I got out first, and then Jason.

"Ladies first," Noah said.

Jason glanced at Noah. I could tell he was trying to calculate a comeback, but he couldn't. I glared at Noah, and he dropped his head with a grin of a twelve-year-old. There was an awkward silence as I found my keys. I looked over my shoulder and saw my past and present looking right back at me. My past was looking at me with a calm expression, while my present looked nothing less than annoyed.

We walked in, and I hung my coat jacket on the coat on a hook before I dropped my bookbag on the futon. I leaned on the radiator to warm up. It was right near the window my bed faced from, and it allowed me to observe the whole apartment from one spot. Jason dropped his stuff on the futon and then went in the fridge to get a water bottle. Noah watched him with questioning eyes. Then he looked at me. It was too quick for me to look away to pretend like I had not been looking at him, so I kept looking. He looked sad before he spoke.

"I should get going. I'll see you later, Nicole," he said before he turned back toward the door.

"Um… see you later man," Jason said.

"Yeah," Noah said before closing the door behind him.

I turned to Jason. He stared at the door for a moment before looking over at me. I could tell he wasn't thrilled. He played with a button on his shirt before he walked over to his bag. I waited for him to start, but he said nothing. That didn't mean the absence of his voice wasn't loud. It made me fidgety, and soon enough, I found myself making a cup of tea to avoid waiting for the inevitable. It's not that I felt like I owed anything to Jason, but we were figuring things out, and this wasn't helping.

"You ok?" I asked when I had enough of the silence.

"Um… yeah... no," he sighed.

"I'm sorry. I should've called you," I said, putting my tea down on the kitchen counter.

"It's ok. I know," he said before kissing my forehead.

I pulled him in for a hug. My chest felt tight with all the stress. He wrapped his arms around me and exhaled deeply. If it were any other situation, I would've felt better. His hugs were the best.

"I actually came here because I found something new about the case. It might be a lead," he said excitedly, and our hug was over.

"What is it?" I asked.

Jason walked over and grabbed his laptop out of his bag. He sat on the futon and patted the small space next to him. I sat and leaned in to see.

"So, do you know a Mrs. Adrienne Strouse?" he asked.

"Yeah. She lives in my town," I said.

"On July 10th, she told the police that she heard an altercation next door at the Crawfords on June 28th. She said she never saw Reginald after that day. She also said that Tracey Crawford, Noah's mom, never left for work that day. Her car was in their driveway the entire time. According to the report, she said she always went to work and never missed a day," Jason said.

My stomach was in a huge knot, and I wondered if there was any information mentioning if I went to their home that day, but I didn't see anything.

"So what does that mean?" I asked.

"Well, I found it interesting. I looked to see if they ever asked Mrs. Strouse anything further, and it was interesting. On July 15th, they went to ask more questions, and she said that she believes she made an error. She refused to give any more information. That's a little fishy. I then went to look up who she was. I found her husband, Zachary Strouse," he said, scrolling through his notes.

"I know that name… I think he got into a car accident or something. It was pretty bad, but he survived," I said.

"Right. Zachary Strouse got into a horrific car accident on July 12th. That was only two days after his wife gave her statement to the investigators," he said.

"That's probably a coincidence," I said.

"No, I don't think so. I looked up information on the car accident, and many people mentioned how Zachary was such a careful driver, but all of a sudden, he got into an accident due to reckless driving. Some friends and family wanted them to investigate and find out if there was something wrong with the car, but the Strouses said no. Then right after, Adrienne refused to make any more statements about the case… something is up," Jason said.

I couldn't argue that there wasn't something odd about the whole thing. My body started to get hot at the thought of Noah having something to do with the accident. He was just a kid at the time. *How could he do something like that*, I thought.

"You think Noah did that? He was sixteen," I said.

"Maybe not him, but someone he knows," Jason said.

"Aren't you scared you'll get into trouble if you get involved in this?" I asked.

"I'm not dropping this. I know that's where you're going with this, and it won't work," Jason said, very matter-of-fact.

This was going to get crazy. I didn't know how, but I knew it would. Like I said, boyfriends were only trouble. You kiss one boy, and all of a sudden, he's getting involved in your ex's criminal background. Okay fine, I know that's not what happened here, but the point is, I was stressed, and I knew this was just the beginning.

Chapter 13

Jason and I had a final at the same time, so we walked to our buildings together. He was just next door. I tried my best to clear my mind of what I had heard the previous night and took my biology final. I was feeling pretty good about it, but I knew I needed to nap the residual stress off. I quickly walked to the little mini-mart on the way back to my apartment and picked up a few groceries. I knew I wasn't supposed to go anywhere but back to the apartment, but not even a stalker was going to have me go hungry.

When I got back to the apartment, I felt my phone vibrating. I saw it was Noah. I answered and put the phone in between my cheek and shoulder.

"Hey, where are you?" his voice asked from the other side of the line.

"I just got back to my apartment," I said, making my way into the kitchen with my two heavy bags.

"I thought you said Jason was going to drop the case," Noah said.

I stopped in my tracks and paused. How could he know?

"What?" I asked.

"Nikki, stop. Don't play the dumb card. You're too smart for that, and it won't work on me… You knew he was still looking into it. I told you it would cause problems," Noah said, and I could hear the stress in his voice.

"What do you expect me to do? I can't control him," I said.

"Well, now you're going to have problems because you're connected to him. Being followed is the least of your issues," he said.

"I thought you said you weren't doing this." I dropped my bags on the counter.

"It's not me," Noah said.

"Then who?" I asked.

Noah laughed a little, and I squeezed my phone so hard in anger, I heard the case make a noise. This was not the time to be laughing. I knew it was probably more out of frustration, but it still made me equally as mad.

"You asshole. You think this is funny." I stomped.

"You think I can just tell you? No. It doesn't work like that." He stopped laughing.

"So I'm just going to be followed? That's it? I'll call the cops," I said.

"If you call the cops, I won't be able to protect you. Open your door. I'm here," he said.

"You're what?" I turned to look at the door. I saw a shadow underneath.

"I'm here. Let me in," he said.

I hung up the phone and saw Noah standing there in an open jacket with a tight muscle shirt and jeans. His hair was ruffled around, but in a sexy way. You would've thought it was early fall, but I could see his nose was a little red. Despite how good he looked, I narrowed my eyes at him and stood by the door so he couldn't come in.

"Why are you here? Don't you have finals to worry about?" I asked.

"I know your little boyfriend hates me, but I figured we would have this conversation in person and not over the phone… I don't know everything yet, and this is safer. And yes, I do," he said, giving the door a little push. I let him in.

"What's going on. Who is after me?" I asked, crossing my arms.

"I can't tell you," he said.

"Noah," I said loudly, and he sighed in response.

He took off his coat and threw it on the futon. I stayed where I was near the door, but he paced around in silence for a few moments.

"I can't tell you who. I just need you to know that I, unfortunately, know some crazy and dangerous people who will protect me at all costs," he said.

"You do not need to be protected from me," I said.

Noah opened his mouth to say something, but then closed it. Instead, he rubbed his jaw and then turned toward me.

"Has he been asking you questions to like verify things or whatever?" he asked.

"Yeah. sometimes." I shrugged, mainly referring to the previous night.

"Maybe you can steer him in the wrong direction," he said.

"No," I said, walking over to my bed and sitting down hard.

"No? Look, I know you don't want to do this, but if I go down, you can too," he said.

"Is that a threat?" I asked with eyes that said *I dare you*.

"No, this is literally the reality of it all," he bit back.

I rubbed my temples and begged myself not to cry from the stress of this and finals. I needed him to leave so I could study. I needed him to leave so I could calm down. I felt my body starting to shake. Everything was becoming way too much.

"Nicole, I'm going to need you to focus here," Noah said, pulling me out of my train of thought.

"I don't know what to do," I said.

Noah sat at the edge of the bed next to me and rubbed his chin as he thought. We had to think of something.

When I finished my last final, Jason celebrated me not being my top level of crazy over school with bringing pizza and Netflix on his laptop. It was the first time ever that we cuddled while we watched a movie. It was nice, just foreign. I hadn't been close to a guy like that since before Noah and I broke up. It didn't feel the same, but it didn't feel bad either. Jason fell asleep, and I watched the movie until it was done. Then it was silent. I looked at his laptop in front of me and was tempted.

I simply touched the touchpad so the computer wouldn't lock. I exited out of the full screen and saw Jason's document with his case notes open. He hadn't spoken about anything for the past week and I wondered why. My curiosity got the best of me. I slipped from his arms and quietly brought the laptop to the futon. His back was turned to me now. I would have time to think of an excuse if he woke up.

I opened the document and scrolled. I stopped and went back up when my eye caught my name, Nicole Smith. There were *paragraphs*. What was going on here? I scanned the words. There was information on when I was questioned. There was information on how close I was to the suspect, meaning Noah. Then, there was the date June 28th with a dash next to it with question marks. He was trying to figure out where I was that day. It was almost as if I was one of his suspects. I was brought into the equation, even after he promised he would not. My stomach and heart fell as I looked up at him. He hadn't stirred.

I held tears back as I read on. He had written down that someone mentioned I visited Noah often and we hung out together almost every day. There was a line that had an asterisk next to it that read, "Nicole Smith was seen leaving her house the early afternoon of the 28th, but it is unknown whether she went to the Crawford residence." I'd had enough. I scrolled back to the beginning of the document and switched to the window that had Netflix open and closed the laptop. I left it on the futon and went to the bathroom and ran cold water on my face and wrists. I tried to steady my breathing, but it took a while. I opened the medicine cabinet and looked at the tiny bottle of pills. I sighed and grabbed it. I placed one on my tongue and swallowed it with some water.

"Nicole," Jason's voice called.

I panicked. I inhaled deeply, held it for a while, and then released the air from my lungs. *Get it together, Nicole. You have to play this off,* I told myself.

"Um… yeah, I'm here," I said, turning off the water.

"You ok?" He yawned.

"Yep… just fine," I said, dabbing the corners of my eyes.

Chapter 14

After taking a day to sleep the stress of finals and my farce of a life off, I packed some of my clothes in my small suitcase. I planned to not be back at my apartment for a few weeks, and while I had a lot of stuff at home, I knew there were some items I couldn't live without. I played music while I folded some shirts. I was bopping to the beat of Ariana Grande's "No Tears Left to Cry", when I heard a knock on the door. I rolled my eyes. I was expecting Jason, but instead, I saw a face I was super happy to see.

"Hey baby," my sister said with a shimmy.

"Rach," I said, opening up my arms.

We hugged and squeezed each other tight. It was then that I realized how fast time was moving. I was used to seeing her multiple times a day, and at this point, I hadn't seen her in almost a month. I let her in, and she looked around while bopping to the music.

"Thanks for coming to pick me up," I said, raising my voice over the music before turning it down.

"You're the only person I'd face Friday Manhattan traffic for." She flashed her eyebrows.

"I love you." I chuckled before going back to folding.

Rachel dropped her bag and coat on the futon before she went to the kitchen to raid the fridge. *What a teenager.* She pulled out some day-old pasta and a bottle of water. She threw the bowl in the microwave.

"So, now that it's over… how was your first semester of college life? Do I have a lot to look forward to?" Rachel asked, leaning on the counter.

"It was definitely an adventure," I deadpanned.

Rachel didn't answer. She brought her food over to my bed and sat down. Her eyebrows were furrowed, and she looked at me with a questioning look. I broke eye contact and went back to folding. She nudged me with her elbow, but I didn't look up. She already knew something was up, but if I dared look her in the eyes I would cry.

"What's wrong, Coco?" she asked.

"Nothing," I said.

"Okay so college clearly didn't teach you the art of being convincing yet," she said, putting her bowl on my nightstand.

I rolled my eyes, but I couldn't help chuckling at that. She smiled triumphantly.

"You have to tell me. I had a feeling something was wrong when you came for Thanksgiving," she said, taking a shirt from my hand and throwing it in the direction of my suitcase just to miss miserably.

"Rachel, please. I can't tell you," I said.

"Is it about Jason?" she asked.

"Yeah, partially," I sighed.

"Hmm… did you guys hook up? Was it disappointing?" she asked.

I turned to look at her and shook my head. I laughed and threw a pillow at her. She laughed and threw it back.

"No, I didn't sleep with him. We're not even official," I said.

"Doesn't mean you can't sleep with him. It's not 1942," Rachel said.

"Rachel," I said, shocked.

"I'm just saying! But what is it? He's so obsessed with you, I doubt he would dare act stupid enough to make you break things off," she said.

"It's complicated," I said.

"You can tell me! I give amazing advice," she said.

"I don't know if I can trust him… and then there's Noah," I sighed.

"Noah? *Noah Crawford?* He's here? What does he have to do with this?" she exclaimed, and I could tell her annoyance toward him was still there. I couldn't blame her.

"Yeah, he goes to school here," I said.

"I don't think you should get involved with him again," she said.

I didn't answer. I started rubbing my temples. Just the thought of it all gave me a headache.

"So you're hooking up with Noah? Okay, this is the tea I live for," she screamed as she leaped off the bed.

"What?" I paused, looking up at her.

"Noah is trouble, but he's super hot. I was jealous you had such a good-looking guy when we were younger," she swooned.

"I'm not sleeping with Noah. I'm not sleeping with anyone," I said.

"Oh. Well, did he ever say anything about the Reggie case?" she asked.

I looked up at her and sighed. I didn't know how to avoid the question without blatantly lying and being obvious. Rachel's eyebrow went up in response to my silence. She was about to start asking questions I did not want to hear when we heard knocking at the door. I rose to get the door, but Rachel was already there. She opened the door and revealed Noah standing there. He looked shocked to see her and she did too.

"Rachel… fancy seeing you here. How's school?" he asked with a small smile.

"Um… good. How's life?" she asked, clearly mocking his awkward tone.

"It's definitely… an adventure," he said, and Rachel looked at me with an exasperated look.

"Hey, Noah… what can I do for you?" I asked, walking toward the door.

His eyes met mine and then he glanced at Rachel to show he didn't want to speak in front of her. I nodded. Rachel looked back between the both of us and then excused herself to the bathroom. I grabbed my keys and followed him out into the hallway.

"Why didn't you text me?" I asked in a low voice.

"I was walking by and figured I would check-in," he said with a smirk as his eyes danced down my body. I looked down at my tank and shorts. Of course, he would see me the one day I never got out of my pajamas.

"Are you confused on where my eyes are?" I asked dryly.

"Anyway… Any updates on Jason and the case?" he asked in almost a whisper with a smirk still on his face.

"He is trying to figure out where I was that day," I sighed.

Noah's expression became serious before it became angry. I looked down. The thought of Jason betraying me was already upsetting. Him finding out that I had anything to do with this would end everything before it even began. Not only with our relationship, but also my whole entire life.

"What a great boyfriend," Noah deadpanned.

"He's not my boyfriend… yet," I said under my breath.

"I suggest reconsidering," Noah said.

"I get it," I bit back.

Noah took a step toward me and leaned on the wall space over my head. I turned away from him and crossed my arms over my chest. He sighed.

"How did you find out?" he asked.

"I looked at his laptop. He has a lot of information on there… unfortunately," I said in a whisper.

Noah nodded and gave me a shocked yet approving look when I looked back at him. I rolled my eyes and created some distance between us. I did not need another episode where Jason saw us together.

"I made sure it was not documented that you came over that day," he said.

"You made sure? Who did your sixteen-year-old self know?" I asked, giving him an incredulous look.

"Like I said, I can't give details, but you should be safe," he said.

"Whatever… thanks, I guess. I have to go back in. Is that all?" I asked, flipping my keys around.

Noah stared at me for a couple seconds before he spoke.

"Turns out I'm going to be in our old town this break," he said smugly.

"Really? Why's that," I said.

"Because something tells me Jason's going to be." Noah shrugged.

"Probably not to see me… Anyway, this makes things a lot more stressful," I sighed, finding the right key for the lock.

"Probably both…his gorgeous girlfriend and the case." He shrugged before turning down the hall.

I opened the door to see Rachel standing right there. She definitely was eavesdropping. She didn't look amused. I stopped and looked back at her once I locked the door.

"I thought you said you had no idea about the case," she said as she put her hands on her hips.

"What do you mean?" I asked, trying to look as calm as possible.

Rachel laughed under breath and gave me an incredulous look. She shook her head and crossed her arms over her chest. She was my height, but that day, she had on boot heels that made her tower over me. I wasn't intimidated, but I could tell she was not thrilled.

"We don't lie to each other, Coco." She stomped.

"Rach, it's really complicated." I put my hand up, stopping her before the lecture started.

"So you... ?" she asked.

"Let's just say I know a lot of things I shouldn't, and Jason looking into this case can cause a lot of problems for Noah and myself," I sighed.

"Then tell him to knock it off. If this is the worst-case scenario, you can literally go to jail. Someone died," she exclaimed.

I nodded with tears on the verge of escaping my eyes. I shrugged. I had no idea what to do.

"So what are you going to do about it?" she asked.

"I have to keep an eye on him and try to mess his investigation up, I guess... It could be really bad if I don't," I said.

"I'm not supposed to know about this, am I?" she asked, and for the first time in a long time, I could hear the fear in my sister's voice.

"No. I can't tell you any more. I shouldn't. It would put you in the same situation I'm in," I said.

"Let me help," she said.

"Are you crazy? I can't ask you to do that," I said.

"You don't have to ask. I'm offering. I know you need help. Your eyes… they scream for help. It's ok. You don't have to do everything alone. I know you have before, but you have me," she said softly.

"It's going to be a lot, and I'm not sure for how long… I don't know. Are you sure?" I asked.

Rachel's eyes looked concerned. I knew she was putting together possible stories in her head. I didn't have time for it. I just needed to know if she was in. I needed her to be my eyes and ears when I couldn't be my own. I needed someone who was not Noah.

"Well yeah, duh. I'm your sister. I'm always on your team," she said.

"This can get dangerous, Rachel. I feel bad getting my little sister in this," I said, pulling my curls into a puff.

"Well, I guess we're even now. We both broke the law," Rachel said.

I slowly turned around to look at her again instead of in the mirror. She widened her eyes at me as if to say "what?".

"What do you mean *we both* broke the law? What have you done? This is *not* what I meant by us needing sister bonding time," I said.

Rachel rolled her eyes and turned on the water to wash her dish. It seemed like she was taking forever but really took less than a minute. Once she dried the dish off, she spoke.

"I mainly mean just sneaking into clubs, or like hooking up with a guy in a car…but I also kind of mean that one time I helped my ex change his grade in the system so he could get that internship," Rachel sighed.

"Great," I deadpanned.

Chapter 15

To celebrate finally being home, I slept for two days straight. Well, I didn't actually sleep for forty-eight hours. I woke up to use the bathroom and eat, but besides that, I slept. I didn't even look at my phone. I needed some time away from being constantly reminded of Jason, Noah, and the case. Rachel was home for the whole weekend, and she acted like everything was normal. I appreciated her for it.

I woke up to Mom kissing me good-bye before she left for work that Monday. I tried to fall back asleep, but I was pretty sure my body had fully charged its battery. I hopped in the shower and sighed happily at the quality water pressure I hadn't felt in a long time. I stood underneath the shower head and let the water wet my hair and run down my body. I moved around so it could massage me everywhere.

The shower is always a great place for one to reevaluate life, but my shower showered you with inspiration. It answered all of life's questions. Not really, but it was a little escape from the hurdles of life. I unintentionally found myself planning my future. I thought of new ways to organize my binder for the next semester, and if I should get a shelf for my apartment, because there had to be a better place for my books than under my futon. I also thought about what exactly to do with Jason. It hurt a little to think about how he was going behind my back after he promised to keep me out of the narrative. I was starting to wonder if that was why he asked me out in the first place—to just use me to find out more, but what was more important was making sure he didn't find any information that led him to find out what I knew.

I decided that I had pruned my skin enough and took off the water. I squeezed as much water out of my curls as possible and wrapped a towel around myself. I hummed as I rubbed some oil into my hair and reached for my blow dryer without looking. My hand hit the marble countertop. It wasn't there. I sighed when I realized it was in my suitcase. I opened the bathroom door and felt an immediate draft. I tightened the towel around me, even though it was going to do nothing for me as far as warmth. I turned the corner and saw someone sitting by the window. I screamed at the top of my lungs and fell back. The person stood up and put their hands out. I paused for a moment and realized it was Noah.

"What the hell are you doing here?" I asked with my voice raw from the scream.

"I... I... Okay, so you weren't answering your phone for the past two days or bell just now. I came up here to see if you were alright," he said with his hands up and eyes opened wide.

"I should call the cops! That's beyond creepy. How did you get up here? Are you crazy? What if someone else was home?" I asked, trying to get up without flashing Noah for a *second* time.

"Only your car was in front of the house and there were none in the driveway," he said, finally lowering his hands.

I shook my head and grabbed some clothes to put on before I slammed the bathroom door behind me. I did my morning routine despite Noah sitting right outside my door and walked out dressed ten minutes later. He was standing by my shelf, looking at an album. Yes, I'm old-fashioned.

"Can you please not touch my stuff?" I asked, walking over to him, just to stop when I realized he was looking at a picture of us from three years before.

"I remember this day," he said with a softness in his voice that I hadn't heard in years.

I got closer to get a look, and he lowered the book so I could see. It was us at Six Flags, hugging each other in front of one of the roller coasters. It had been our physics trip there. It was also my birthday weekend. I remembered every moment of that trip. It was the first time I had spent the night away from my parents. It was the first time I spent the night with a boy. Things had gotten more serious in our relationship.

"Yeah. I do too," I said, sounding more sentimental than I wanted to.

Noah flipped through a few pictures quickly and stopped on my prom photos. I wore a white and gold dress.

It was form-fitting on top and opened up on the bottom into a short train. It was beautiful. I usually thought I looked decent most days, but that night, I felt like a goddess.

"You look beautiful. Was this junior or senior prom?" he asked, running his fingers over the pictures slowly.

"Senior prom," I said.

He looked at me and then looked back down at the pictures like he was looking for something. I looked at the pictures quizzically.

"What?" I asked finally.

"You don't have any pictures of your date," he said.

"I didn't have one," I said before walking over to my desk chair to sit.

Noah gave me an incredulous look and then scoffed.

"You turned everyone down?" he asked.

"I got asked by two guys, and I didn't want to go with either of them." I shrugged.

"So, wait, what happened at junior prom? Did you take a boyfriend?" he asked.

"I didn't go," I said.

"Your boyfriend didn't want to?" he asked, clearly trying to get answers.

"I didn't have one," I said.

"Oh," he said, and I could see that he was pleased even though he was trying to hide it.

"Did you have a girlfriend? Let me guess. Yes," I said.

"Nothing serious, no," he said, leaning back and crossing his arms.

"So, what does that mean? You would sleep with them and then dump them?" I asked.

"Nikki, you know me. That's not my thing. There was one girl earlier this year, but I realized I wasn't ready for something serious," he said.

"Oh," I said.

"Yeah. So… you still hold the record for my only girlfriend," he said with a shrug.

"What about that girl that was a junior when we were freshmen? You dated her before me."

"Miranda? Honestly, in the end, she just wanted to hookup. I didn't know what hit me." He shrugged with a smirk.

"Ew," I said.

"Not necessarily. I definitely learned a lot during those couple months," he said with a reminiscent smirk that made me involuntarily roll my eyes.

I stood up at that remark and put my hands on my hips. I'd had enough of that. One thing I never wanted to hear, not two years before and not at that moment, was him being with some other girl. I was not the jealous type at all, but there had to be limits.

"Well, I'm okay so you can leave now," I said.

"But you were undoubtedly the most real and most important thing I have ever been a part of," Noah said softly.

I hated him so much at that moment. Okay, not really, but I hated how it made me melt a little. I had been doing so well with not feeling a thing, and now that was all going down the drain. I told myself that I was having the worst case of nostalgia, and I wasn't actually feeling new emotions, but instead, I was missing the ones I used to feel from this person. It was like when you watched an old TV show from your childhood. You enjoy it more for the memories of how it made you feel when things were different; before the world made you who you were now.

"Thank you… Um, but I'm okay now like I said so you can go," I struggled as I looked down at the white carpet instead of him.

"Yeah… right," Noah said, standing up.

We were halfway downstairs when I heard the bell ring. I ran down the remaining stairs and checked the monitor by the coat closet to see who was at the door. It was Jason.

"Shit." I stomped.

"Wow. Two curses in an hour. College is changing you," Noah snickered, walking up behind me.

"It's Jason. You can't be here," I whispered.

He bit his lip before running back up the stairs. I made a whispered scream and waved my arms.

"Where are you going?" I whispered.

"To hide up here," he called and then was gone.

I groaned and straightened my clothes before I opened the door. I plastered a fake smile on my face.

"Hey, what are you doing here?" I asked cheerfully.

"Hi, gorgeous! I didn't think I could miss you so much after just a few days," he said before leaning in to kiss me by surprise.

I wanted so badly to roll my eyes. I knew that was most likely a lie. I kept the smile on my face and stepped aside to let him in. He spun around a couple times before looking inside the living room in awe.

"Your house is beautiful," he said in shock.

"Thanks. It's just home to me." I shrugged.

"Your parents must be loaded," he said, walking toward the kitchen.

I made a mental note to thank Noah for deciding to hide upstairs. When Jason finally got past the initial shock of my home, I got him to sit down in the living room while I made us tea. I was the farthest thing from a coffee person, so I didn't attempt to even touch Dad's french press that I never learned how to use. It was amazing how much of an expert I was in breaking things. I was not going to risk him disowning me. Jason would have to settle with tea.

When I got back to the living room, Jason was looking at the picture frames that sat on the table next to the couch. There were mostly pictures of Rachel and myself in our younger years. I was too on edge to be embarrassed about him looking at them.

"You and your sister look a lot alike now, but as kids, you guys must have been mistaken for twins all the time," he exclaimed.

"Yeah, we were," I said with a chuckle.

Rachel and I might as well have been twins. We looked very much alike and were only fourteen months apart. We both had the same milk chocolate skin and were both on the shorter side and smaller. She always expressed how she wished her face was more proportioned like mine. I never really got what she meant, though. She was beautiful and had a fun personality to accentuate it. She got that from Dad. They both always spoke like they were on the verge of a punchline. Meanwhile, I was the more quiet and reserved one, like Mom. I'm not sure where I got the sarcasm from. Maybe that was uniquely mine.

I set down his tea on the coffee table and then sat down next to Jason, who was still examining the photos. I tried to look as calm as possible, but on the inside, I was wondering what Noah was doing upstairs. I didn't want him looking through my stuff. Not that I currently had anything to hide from him. The person who I wanted to hide everything from was sitting right next to me, rambling about how much he already missed being free in his apartment instead of home.

"How about you? Everything ok? You didn't answer your phone," he said before taking a long sip of tea.

"Yeah, I'm fine. I've been sleeping a lot. I needed to just destress." I shrugged as I thought about how I would possibly destress from this.

"I was a little worried, but yeah I get that. I sat around at home, doing nothing, and it felt pretty good," he said.

I wondered if he was telling the truth. Did he really do nothing, or did he just mean nothing for school? I had a hard time believing he hadn't looked at anything related to the case. I was waiting for him to mention it. I knew it was coming.

"I'm surprised. You're always working on something," I said.

"I know, but after all I had found out a few days ago, I just felt a little overwhelmed and burnt out," he said with more seriousness in his tone.

I put my cup down as I thought about what he said. There were so many things he could have found out. I exhaled deeply to stay calm. I had to play this part. I had to act like I was oblivious to everything.

"What did you find out?" I asked nonchalantly.

Jason looked down at his cup for a while. He didn't answer me immediately, and that made me nervous. I was holding my breath.

"So… It's a lot. You should sit do—*stay seated* for this," he sighed.

Chapter 16

An hour and two more cups of tea later, and I had heard everything that Jason dug out of the catacombs of the Crawfords' lives. My head hurt, and my stomach was in my throat at the thought of Noah walking downstairs and losing it on him.

Jason explained that he started with digging up information on the Strouses. He was completely positive that the Crawfords had something to do with Zachary Strouse's accident. Zachary Strouse drove a computer-controlled car by Blue Crown motors. Blue Crown motors, apparently, was a company under the supervision of Carter Craig Telecommunications, also known as CCT Network —the huge company in which Tracey Crawford was an executive. There had been talk of CCT Network hacking into cars and killing its high profile owners, but when it got too much publicity, CCT bought out one of the detective agencies, and the topic was dropped almost immediately, due to some lame explanation about tainted evidence.

Jason also said that there have been references to files that he had been trying to find, but many of them are no longer in existence. Someone had tampered with the evidence. That led him to find other cases in the area that were never solved, or had outcomes that did not make much sense. There weren't many, but there was one that stood out. It was from six years ago, and it involved the death of Carter Crawford, Noah's father. He was found dead in his office. The autopsy stated that he had died from a sudden heart attack. Many friends and neighbors of the Crawfords reported that Carter was in perfect health and was into taking care of himself. What was interesting was the Crawfords never pushed to have the matter further looked at. This all happened just two months after Carter wanted to announce some 'expanded business ventures'. It wasn't specified how he wanted to expand exactly.

"This is crazy," I said, rubbing my temples.

"That it is…," Jason sighed.

"So now what?" I asked.

"Well, now we have good reason to believe Zachary Strouse's accident was the result of foul play. We know that the Crawfords probably played with evidence," he said.

"Right, but that doesn't explain who killed Reggie," I said.

"No, but the Strouses probably know more. Maybe I can speak to them," he said.

"So you're going to do what? *Ding-dong*, hi, can you tell me what you know about the case that almost killed you when you told the authorities what you knew," I deadpanned.

"I have a plan." He gave me a smug look.

I walked upstairs to my room to put on warmer clothes. I expected to see Noah there, but he was nowhere in sight. I figured he had climbed out of the window when

I didn't see any texts from him on my phone. I pulled off my t-shirt and walked up to my closet to find a sweater. When I slid the already ajar closet door to the side, Noah fell out on me. I lost my balance, and we hit the floor with a loud thud.

"Get off," I said in a loud whisper.

"Sorry. I didn't know you were going to open the door," he said in an equally loud whisper.

I heard some footsteps outside my bedroom door and then a knock. Noah and I looked at each other with wide eyes. He sprang up and looked around before running toward the bathroom. He stopped before he walked in and gave me a once over.

"You forgot your shirt," he said softly before closing the bathroom door in.

There was a knock again.

"Hey, Nicole? It sounded like someone fell," Jason said from the other side of the door to the hallway.

I ran over to it and opened it a crack, just so he could see my face and nothing else. He stretched his neck to see if he could see more, but I could tell by his look of disappointment that he was not successful.

"I'm fine. I... I knocked over my suitcase. Everything is fine. I'll be downstairs in ten minutes," I said before closing the door.

I pressed my ear to the door to hear his footsteps go slowly down the stairs before I walked back farther into my room. I opened the door to the bathroom and pulled the shower curtain to the side. Noah was sitting in the tub.

"Why did you sit in the tub?" I chuckled.

"Because I'm taller than the shower curtain," he said, clearly annoyed.

"He's gone. I need you to leave when we leave the house. I can't have my parents seeing you," I said, turning to a serious subject.

Noah gave me a small frown. My parents didn't hate him like how his mother hated me for the sheer fact that I existed, but they were wary of him at times. He wasn't a bad boy, but he was definitely more popular in high school than I was. Everyone knew him, and every girl pined after him. Mom was worried I would get my heartbroken. I guess she was right about that.

She was also worried that we wouldn't be able to relate to each other because he's white and I'm black. I didn't really care about that. All I wanted was for him to acknowledge me for who I really was—a black girl. He might not have thought it was a big deal, and it wasn't to us when we were alone, but society would constantly remind us that we were different. People would look at me differently than they would at him as a white guy. I didn't want the "I don't see color" or "We're only one race, the human race" type of conversations. I wanted him to know that we were different and still want me just as much.

Dad was just worried like a typical father was. I hadn't dated before. I was this fourteen-year-old, naive girl who was diving headfirst into a relationship with a guy who had a lot more experience. Noah soon proved himself to them, and he became part of our family. That was until the incident. When Noah became a suspect, my parents suggested we spend less time together, which pretty much involved me asking if we could go out and them saying no.

"We wouldn't want that, would we," he said with a smirk, but it wasn't convincing. I knew it hurt him.

"Thanks for checking up on me," I said, trying to hide the unwelcome sympathy in my voice

"Of course… you should put on clothes," he said with a flash of his eyebrows.

I looked down and realized I only had on a bra. I was mortified. I ran to the closet and put on a sweater quickly. Noah slowly walked out of the bathroom with his hands in his pockets.

"I'm so sorry," I said, smoothing down the tight bun I put my hair in after the shower.

"Nothing I haven't seen," he said with another smirk crawling up on his lips.

I stopped in my tracks and just looked at him. I gave him a look that dared him to say more, but he was smart this time. I grabbed my purse on my chair before rolling my eyes at his boyish grin. I waved bye to remind him that he needed to leave and closed my bedroom door.

I wasn't thrilled about going to the Strouses for multiple reasons. The biggest being that Mrs. Strouse used to wave to me from next door when I would visit Noah. I prayed that the past couple of years really aged her or really aged me, and she wouldn't recognize who I was. I knew I was asking for a lot though. I went and put on an optimistic smile to play the role of supportive-kind-of-girlfriend.

"Is that Noah's old house? Jesus, you guys are living large here," Jason said, looking over at the gray and black house next to the Strouses.

"Yeah... Big houses in the middle of nowhere." I chuckled.

We rang the Strouses doorbell and waited for them to answer. Jason looked completely at ease, but I was the exact opposite. The door opened, and Mrs. Strouse appeared from behind it. She was an older white woman with brown hair with one silver streak. Her gray eyes were kind, even though her perfectness made her seem intimidating. She took an approving look at Jason and straightened her dress. Then her eyes lingered on me before she smiled.

"Hi. How can I help you?" she asked.

"Hi, Mrs. Strouse. I intern with the Success Gazette and am doing a piece on families who support amazing causes and are involved in your communities like you and your husband. Would you mind if we asked you and your husband some questions?" Jason asked without missing a beat. It was a little scary how good he was at that.

"Well, that is so kind. Come on in out of the cold," she said softly.

We walked into a large entryway with two spiral staircases that lead to the second floor. I looked closely and realized one wasn't a staircase at all and instead was a ramp. It was probably for Mr. Strouse's wheelchair. Mrs. Strouse led us into a big living room and told us to take a seat while she went to get some refreshments and look for Mr. Strouse.

Jason seemed at ease through all of this. He looked like he was supposed to be there even though the reality was just the opposite. It made me wonder at what other times was he acting and could I really trust him. I was going to say something to him when Mr. Strouse wheeled in. He had on jeans and a button-down. His hair was an even silver like he got it done that way. He smiled at us both.

"Hey. You guys are interns?" Mr. Strouse asked warmly.

"Um… he is," I replied.

"Moral support? I like it. You're one of the Smith girls, right?" he asked, squinting his eyes knowingly.

"I am. Nice to see you again." I smiled.

"I knew I recognized you! Nicole, you have grown so much," Mrs. Strouse said, walking in with a tray of oatmeal cookies and bottles of water.

"How have you been, Mrs. Strouse?" I asked.

"Same old, same old." She waved.

"I just wanted to ask about your charity support," Jason said, getting everyone back on topic.

"Ask away. It's what I spend my free time tending to," Mr. Strouse said.

"Your foundation, Success from Success… where did you get your inspiration to found it from?" Jason asked.

"I grew up a poor kid. I wanted to make sure that the price of college wouldn't be a reason for someone not to go. Every year, we take nominations from teachers in struggling neighborhoods and we choose to pay the full four-year tuition of ten students a year," Mr. Strouse said.

"That's amazing. Is this in partnership with other businesses in the area?" Jason asked.

"Yes, a few," Mrs. Strouse answered.

"I know the CCT Network has donated to charities in the past. Have you been one of them?" Jason asked.

Both Mr. and Mrs. Strouse were silent at that. I made sure to not make eye contact with either one of them. This was already so uncomfortable for me. I folded my hands in my lap to ensure they would not shake. After a very long and uncomfortable moment of silence, Mr. Strouse finally spoke.

"We don't work with the table… I mean the CCT Network anymore. We had differences in practice so we made partnerships elsewhere," Mr. Strouse said, and I could hear something that sounded like fear in his voice.

Chapter 17

I was glad that Jason did not overstay his welcome and got the hint that asking questions about the Crawfords was uncomfortable for the Strouses. I did not want to burn a bridge that could have easily been burned in the past, considering I dated a possible criminal. The last thing I wanted was problems with anyone in town. We took the scenic route back to my house as we spoke about what he heard from the Strouses.

"So we didn't find out anything," I said, rolling down the window and letting the cold air hit my burning face.

"What are you talking about? We totally did," Jason said.

"And that was what? Mr. Strouse cares about the less fortunate?" I asked.

"Yeah that, but we also found out he refers to CCT as The Table. Have you ever heard of that before?" he asked.

"I don't think so… I thought he made a mistake when he said that," I said, leaning back as I thought about it.

"I don't think it was," Jason said softly.

Something told me he was right. I knew I would have to tell Noah about this. I sighed as I thought about how messy this situation was and how there was no way for me to get out of it. I wondered if this is how people who committed crimes felt—always trying to clean up the never-ending messes they got themselves into.

"So, question…," Jason said with unsureness in his voice.

"What's up?" I asked, turning to him.

"The authorities seem to think something may have happened to Reggie at the Crawford house on June 28th of that year… What was it like at the Crawford house? Did you go visit often?" Jason asked.

I thought about the question over and over in my head. Ever since I had seen his laptop, I wondered if he would ask what I was doing that day. He hadn't asked that yet, but something told me it would be coming soon. I realized I had been taking too long to answer when Jason glanced over at me.

"I would go over sometimes, and he would come over to me other times. His house was pretty normal… Nothing was unusual," I said, trying to sound as nonchalant about the answer as possible.

"Do you remember June 28th of that year? Did something seem up to you? Did you see him that day?" he asked.

I took a moment to remember what I had told the authorities. I had a feeling Jason was checking to see if I was going to say the same thing as I said two years ago. A rush of disappointment engulfed me with a concentration on my chest.

"That was just a couple weeks into vacation. I think I rode my bike and had some ice cream with friends. Noah was there." I shrugged before looking out the window.

It took everything in me to hold back my tears. Jason promised he would not get me involved in this, and he had broken that promise.

"Alright. Well, here you are. I should head home before it gets dark. I'll call you tonight," Jason said as he pulled up to my house.

He leaned in for a kiss after he hugged me, but I acted like I didn't realize. He let me down, and I was not happy. I unlocked my door, but before I could completely get in he honked his horn. I turned around to see him waving. I waved back.

I was happy to find every hiding spot in my room free of Noah. I changed into a t-shirt and shorts and went into the kitchen for something to eat. I was heating up some of Dad's leftover chicken and rice from the night before when I heard the front door open along with the jingling of keys.

"I'm home," Rachel's voice called.

"In the kitchen," I called back.

Rachel walked in with her booster uniform on. She had switched her white sneakers for her black Uggs for the ride home. She ran up to me and hugged me warmly.

"I missed seeing you here," she said before dropping her bookbag on one of the kitchen island stools.

"I missed being home. The apartment is just not this," I said as I reached into the microwave to grab my plate.

Rachel ran out of the kitchen and came back barefoot. She opened the pantry and grabbed a long packet of crackers. I mentally estimated that they would be gone in fifteen minutes tops. We were around the same size, but Rachel always had a crazy appetite. She was never not hungry.

"Mom said she and Dad aren't coming home until late, so we can order whatever we want," Rachel said, swiping on her phone with one hand and feeding her mouth crackers with the other.

"As long as it's not pizza or Chinese food, I'm ok," I said.

"Why?" she asked.

"That's all I would order at school." I chuckled.

"Let's go out and eat then," she said.

"Can it wait a couple hours though?" I asked looking down at my finished plate.

"Yeah. I get to pick the place since you're making me wait," Rachel said with a small shrug and smirk.

I shrugged in agreement. I went back to eating and thinking about my farce of a day, *correction*, my farce of a life, when I caught Rachel staring at me.

"What?" I asked, standing up to put my dish in the dishwasher.

"I don't know. I just get the feeling something is wrong." Rachel shrugged.

"Yeah, like everything," I sighed.

"What did Noah do?" she asked dryly.

"Noah snuck in the house today through my bedroom window like it's sophomore year of high school, but he's currently not even the problem," I started.

"He what? And I knew it! I would ask you if he was over in your room and you said no! Liar," she exclaimed with an amused look on her face.

"Whatever… The main issue is… Jason came over, and we ended up going to the Strouses to get some questions answered. Then he started asking me questions. He also has leads… So yeah, I'm not having the best of days," I said.

"Shit. That's crazy. What are you going to do?" she asked.

"I'm not sure yet," I said.

Rachel decided on Antonio's. It was an upscale Italian-American fusion restaurant that people would travel to from all parts of New York to eat the overpriced, yet undoubtedly perfect, pasta dishes. I threw on a form-fitting black dress with a v-neckline. I wore my white faux fur jacket with it. It had been a while since I had dressed up, and I was admiring myself in the mirror when Rachel walked downstairs in a matching pink blazer and pants. I brought my shoulder up to my chin and gave her an approving look.

"You ready to party?" she asked.

"I don't know if this really counts as partying, but sure." I chuckled before I followed her out the door.

Rachel drove so I had a chance to text Noah. I had to tell him what Jason's ideas were. Jason could've been wrong, but if he wasn't then Noah needed to know sooner rather than later. I had no idea what to do, so I needed his help regardless.

Nicole Smith: He might have some dangerous leads. Call me at 11

I clicked away from his name and texted Michelle, who wanted to confirm the plans we had for the next day. I said yes absentmindedly. Ten minutes later, Noah texted me back.

Noah Crawford: What do you mean dangerous?

Nicole Smith: Dangerous as in the last ten minutes of Law and Order, but we're the criminals.

There was no answer to that. I put my phone away when we drove up to the restaurant. Rachel parked, and we walked in. It was after seven so the lights had already been dimmed, and the jazz band was already playing their tunes. I was taking in my surroundings when Rachel pulled me into a corner. It all happened so fast that I felt dizzy.

"What are you doing?" I asked.

"I know that woman. I don't know how I know that face, but it gives me a bad feeling," Rachel said looking over my shoulder.

I turned and looked around the corner. Then my eyes fell on a woman with pale skin and long black hair. Her cheekbones were very prominent, and her eyes looked like ones that I knew all too well. It was Tracey Crawford. I gasped and turned back to face Rachel.

"Who is she?" Rachel asked.

"Noah's mom," I answered.

"Ooo wasn't she like... a bitch?" Rachel asked way too loud.

"Okay first, way too loud. Second, yes. She was not a fan of me, and I wasn't trying too hard to be her friend either," I said.

"Sorry. Do you want to leave?" she asked.

I thought about it for a moment. What was Tracey going to really do? I finally met eyes with Rachel, whose eyes were bulging. I gave her a confused look before I felt a hand on my shoulder.

"Hey. We need to talk," Noah's voice said.

Chapter 18

So now we get to the part of the story where I ended up in a gender-neutral bathroom with my ex-boyfriend, so we could speak candidly for a couple minutes without his mother seeing us because she hated my very existence. This was definitely one of the lower points of my life. Each stall was an actual room with a door that reached the ground. This allowed for privacy, but also for no personal space at all. I leaned on one side, but of course, Noah confidently stood in the middle.

"Don't look at me like that," I said.

"Like what?" he smugly asked, looking appreciatively at my dress.

"Like that. Stop checking me out," I said, crossing my arms and looking to the side.

"Who said I was doing that?" he chuckled.

"Unfortunately, you're not very discrete. Anyway, I have news on Jason," I said.

"Alright. How dangerous is the stuff he claims he knows?"

"On a scale of one through ten, I would assume eight or nine."

"Okay. What was it?" he asked calmly, but I could see the concern in his eyes.

"That your family is corrupt and caused the Strouse accident because of the statement Mrs. Strouse shared. Also, what's The Table?" I asked after explaining.

Noah's face went straight, and he looked scared. He took a step near me and leaned in toward my ear. I could smell his cologne. He had on just the right amount. I stopped breathing at the proximity.

"*Please don't say that out loud*. I don't need people knowing you know," he said softly in my ear.

"What is it? Why can't I say it," I whispered back.

"Just trust me on this one," he said.

I just stared at him for a moment. I could tell he was being serious, instead of the usual smug he was. Something was wrong, and he was about to say something when there was a knock on the door. We ignored it at first, thinking the person would get the point and move to the next stall, but they knocked again. Noah and I looked at each other for a moment as if we both assumed the other knew who it was.

"Someone is in here," Noah called.

"Noah Carter Crawford, open the door," a woman's voice called from the other side of the door.

Noah and I both looked at each other. I knew that voice. A sour taste came to my mouth. Noah's expression confirmed my suspicions. I opened the door slowly to reveal Tracey Crawford standing there with her arms crossed over her chest. She gave him a questioning look before her eyes fell on me and narrowed. Noah's stance had completely changed, and instead of the confident man I was used to seeing, he looked like a scared child.

"So… that's what you've been doing," she said, looking from him to me.

"Hi, Mrs. Crawford," I said in a voice that was so small, I almost couldn't hear myself.

"Nicole… causing trouble once again, I hear. How are you dear," she said accusingly.

"I'm alright," I said.

I looked over at Noah, whose eyes were already on me. His expression was painfully sad. It was the type of sad I would never wish on my worst enemies.

"Mom, I have to speak to Nicole. I'll be out soon," he said in a voice that made it seem like he was asking more than telling her.

"If you must… Five minutes and please do not… no canoodling." She shivered, giving me a grossed-out look before closing the door back.

Noah sighed and said something underneath his breath. I didn't ask him what it was. I assumed it had something to do with his mom being a raging bitch. He looked embarrassed.

"I'm sorry about that," he said softly.

"Not your fault. So… Jason," I said, bringing up the subject again.

"I have to say… I actually don't know how to handle this." Noah shrugged with a stressed laugh. It was the kind of laugh that came out when things were so hopeless that all you could do was laugh and pray that it would make it hurt less. I stopped and just looked at him. I wasn't expecting that answer. I wanted a plan, and he didn't give one.

"We can't just give up," I said.

"I know, but… you want a plan in which we keep Jason safe and stop him at the same time. I don't know… wait… no," he said in a low voice.

"No, tell me. What is it," I pressed.

"We need to knock him off of his trail. Not in an obvious way, but we need to be one step ahead of him at all times," he said, rubbing his chin while he thought.

"Okay, so we have to find a small way to sabotage this investigation that will have big effects," I whispered to myself.

"We just have to do this without people knowing," Noah said.

"Clearly. I wouldn't tell anyone." I gave him an incredulous look.

"No, I mean… certain people. The people who are watching you and Jason," Noah said.

I paused and looked at him with my mouth open, but unable to formulate words. I shook my head and put my hand up to stop him from saying anything else. I knew it wasn't his fault, but I hated that he wouldn't tell me who these people were. I ran my hands over my dress to keep them from smacking him.

"I'm going to go before I'm given more reason to not like you. We'll finish talking about this later," I said, reaching for the stall's knob.

"Okay. I'll call you," Noah said with a small smile.

"Unless my phone is tapped…," I said, but it was more of a question.

"No. It's not," he said.

"Alright, then yeah, call me later," I said in a slightly annoyed tone.

"Nicole."

"Yes?"

"You really do look beautiful tonight... Jason is an idiot to break your trust and put you through this again," he said.

"Stop making this a Noah versus Jason thing," I said, reaching for the knob again.

"No, wait. It's not. I'm sorry. It's not like that at all. I… never mind. I just want you to know that if I could make this all go away for you… I would. I feel like it's my fault every day," he said as he stood in front of the door.

I didn't know what to say besides "thank you". Noah got out the way so I could open the door. When we opened the door, there was a tall girl fluffing her long auburn hair in the mirror. She just glanced at me at first, but then glared when she saw Noah come out after me.

"Noah, I've been wondering where you went," she said.

"Eliza… I told you I was coming back," Noah said in an annoyed but polite voice.

"Who's she?" the girl, apparently named Eliza, asked in the rudest way possible.

Noah's eyes fell on me in the mirror. His eyes wouldn't leave mine like he was trying to tell me something, but I couldn't tell what.

"Hi. I'm Nicole. Nice to meet you. What's your name?" I asked in the most polite tone I could fake.

Her eyes widened for a moment. I turned back to Noah in the mirror, and he looked pale. Eliza was glaring at him, and her nails tapped quickly on the marble countertop.

"Eliza Craig… So, *you're the ex*," Eliza said.

There was something about the way Eliza said that sentence that did not sit well with me. Something told me she knew way more about me than I knew about her, which was hardly anything. Noah's expression also did not help.

"Are you his girlfriend?" I asked.

At the same time, Noah answered "no" and Eliza answered "yes". I put my hands up at how ridiculous it sounded and how uncomfortable it made me feel. I turned to Noah, not in the mirror, but in person this time. He had his hands in his pockets and looked at me with the same fear in his eyes he had just looked at his mother with.

"We're not a couple," he said annoyed.

"Oh Noah, don't be silly. You sure like to act like my boyfriend when—" she began.

"Please give it a rest, Eliza," Noah cut her off.

I raised an eyebrow at Noah as I backed up toward the bathroom door. He looked like he wished he could melt into the floor.

"So… you're sleeping with her," I said accusingly.

"No… I… we… It happened once, and then I told her I couldn't," he said.

"Short story, slightly longer… We reconnected a couple years ago. Noah was still not over his little Nikki. *Blah blah blah.* I told him I could help him get over you, and when I finally get to some progress, look who he runs into at school... Are you following? If not, it's you. *Little Miss Perfect,* who can never ever do anything wrong, even when you're literally doing everything wrong," she said, crossing her arms.

I nodded slowly. The only thing that could leave my lips was a sigh. First, that was too much information. Second, this was not the time I wanted to process Noah still having feelings for me. It would be too much.

"I have to go," I said, running out of the bathroom before anyone could say anything else.

I walked out into the dining room and found Rachel sitting down in a booth alone. She had already started her meal. She gave me a frown.

"I was starting to wonder if you were doing more than talking in there," Rachel said dryly before uncovering a plate of linguine alfredo.

"Please, Rach. Not now," I said before sitting down.

"I'm just kidding around. I even got you your favorite," she said, gesturing toward my plate.

"Thanks," I said before taking a bite of my fish.

"What happened in there?" she asked.

"I'll tell you in a little." I exhaled as I saw Noah, Eliza, Tracey, and some other tall, bald man leaving the restaurant.

Once we got in the car, I updated Rachel of everything that had happened. I told her that I needed to figure out a game plan for Jason. I also added that I was being watched, and Noah knew who was doing it, but wouldn't tell me. Of all the important issues at hand, she asked the most irrelevant question.

"So… since Jason is kind of a jerk, are you going to get back with Noah? Lookin' like a damn model today in that suit!" She screamed as we sped down the highway.

"You're impossible," I sighed, rubbing my temples.

"No, you are if you don't think this through. A beautiful guy can't get over you. It's been two years. He like loves you! I wish I had that. Don't be dumb," she said.

I sat up at that and turned to her in the dark of the night. Only the light of the stereo and the streetlights allowed me to see small fragments of her face.

"What will be dumb is if I focus on that when I could literally go to fucking jail if I don't figure this out," I bit.

Rachel was quiet for a while. I didn't mean to scream at her, but I needed her to stay on task if she was going to help me.

"I'm sorry, Coco. We'll figure this out. I promise," she said softly.

By the time we got home, I felt bad for snapping at Rachel. I hugged her after we pulled into the driveway. I wanted to cry it out because of how stressed I was, but I was so stressed that I felt like I couldn't cry. There was just so much to do and crying would just take time away from that.

When we got home, Mom and Dad were sitting in the living room. Dad was still in his scrubs and Mom was still in her white coat. They had just gotten home. Dad stood up with a tired smile and gave us both a hug. Mom followed. Moments like these didn't happen much since I moved to the city for school. I missed it. At that moment, what I missed, even more, were the times when hugs from Mom and Dad could fix everything. I couldn't help but think that moments of being together like this might not happen for much longer if I didn't figure out what to do with all of this mess.

Chapter 19

Unless there was an emergency, Tuesdays meant that Dad would be home. If Rachel and I had off from school or had a short day, Dad would take us out for lunch, and we would get whatever we wanted. It was usually something super unhealthy that Mom would not be a fan of–she was definitely the strict one. Dad was only tough on us when he had no other choice.

It was a Tuesday. Before I went to bed the night before, I told myself I would ask Dad if he wanted to get lunch like old times, even though Rachel would be in class. I missed spending time with him, and I wanted to get as much time in as possible–just in case. What I did not expect was to see him in my room at eight in the morning, waking me up.

"Dad… no, it's too early," I groaned, putting my head under my pillow.

"I'm sorry baby, but you got a delivery," he said.

"I don't care. I don't want it," I whined.

"It might be worth getting up for," he said.

I pulled the pillow away from my face and opened one eye to look at him. He had an amused look on his face. He yawned as he stretched in his robe and pajamas before he gestured toward my door. I rolled my eyes and nodded. *It better be good*, I thought. All the ways I would show an attitude if it was, in fact, not good enough ran through my head as I walked to the bathroom.

I washed up and came downstairs in a tank and yoga pants. I first walked into the kitchen to see a ridiculously big bouquet of flowers in a beautiful glass vase in the middle of the kitchen island. Dad was reading the note attached to it when I got there. He looked up at me with a questioning look. I walked over and read over his shoulder. The note read:

To my movie… I'm sorry. - Noah

I gave a loud groan before I put the kettle on.

"What is *this* sorry for?" Dad asked.

"I don't even know where to begin," I sighed.

"I thought you lost contact with him," he said.

"He goes to NYU," I sighed.

"Ohhh… Well, I always liked Noah. He was a nice guy, and it was clear he was really in love with you. That whole Reginald Crawford case made things very messy though... Not that I think he did it," he said uneasily.

"I know, Dad," I sighed again.

"So, you two are…," he began.

"We're just friends," I said, cutting him off.

"Okay," he said with his hands up before walking out and back to his office.

The doorbell rang, and I walked over to the door to answer it. I opened the door to a very happy Michelle, who was there with her arms stretched ready to embrace me. She engulfed me in a hug that was very cold from her time being outside. I stepped aside and let her in to be nice, but I was kicking myself on the inside because I had forgotten I had made plans with her for the day. I never minded seeing my best friend, but the problem was I had more important plans for the day.

"Why aren't you dressed?" she asked.

I cursed myself in my head and tried to think of an excuse. It was hard for me to lie in general. It was even harder to lie to someone who had known me for over ten years. Michelle was sharp and there was not much you could get past her.

"I'm not feeling too well," I sighed with an apologetic smile.

"Oh no. Why?" she asked.

"Um… my head hurts mostly. I think I had too much to drink last night," I sighed.

"Oh… a hangover? I, unfortunately, have become *way* too familiar with that feeling. How much did you drink?" she asked as she took off her hat and coat.

"I don't know… like a bottle of wine," I said.

"Holy shit. You're like two pounds! Why would you do that? I told you to always alternate with water," she said, rustling her corkscrew curls and throwing her coat into the closet. Yes, I mean literally throwing it in the closet without a hanger. I no longer even bothered to fight her on it.

"I don't know." I shrugged.

"Let's get you upstairs. You probably want to lay down," she said, pushing me toward the stairs. Her mother-mode was on.

Michelle told me to get in bed and went back downstairs to make me a cup of tea. I heard my phone chime, but I ignored it. For a moment, I listened to my friend's advice and enjoyed the comfort of my bed, even though I wasn't sick at all. Michelle soon came back up with my largest mug filled with tea. It was the one she had gotten me that was purple and said "I am the boss". I sipped the tea but couldn't help but look at the clock on my wall. It was still early, but I knew I had things I needed to do.

"How does it feel to be done?" I asked her.

"Good," she sighed. It was not convincing.

"What's wrong?" I asked.

"I got a C- in a class," she said.

I didn't mean to, but I gasped. Michelle had never taken school as seriously as I did, but that was more because she was one of those people who would just do well without trying. While I had moments where I would do well without studying too, they happened far more often for her than me. I could see the uneasiness in her eyes.

"What happened?" I asked.

"I just got caught up with other things." She shrugged.

I knew what the other things were. She meant her sister's friends and their parties. Michelle's sister, Meghan, had always been into the party scene. She was super popular and would probably rather be caught dead than miss a party. She made Rachel look boring. I knew from the moment Michelle mentioned all the parties she had started going to, that it would be a distraction. It was a huge change than what Michelle was used to. She was trying to keep up. I wondered if I had more time to worry about other things if I would have said anything about it.

"I'm sure if you put more time toward studying next semester, you'll make it up," I said.

"Yeah, I guess," she said before my phone chimed on my desk.

Before I could get up, Michelle walked over to my phone to bring it over to me. She glanced at the screen for half of a second, but of course, knowing my luck that was enough for her to see who the notification was from. It was Noah. I knew it before she said it. She stopped walking and just stood in the middle of the room.

"You're speaking to Noah now?" she asked with narrowed eyes.

"Um... I... He goes to NYU now," I said.

"He gave you the flowers downstairs," she almost screamed.

"Can you please not read my notifications?" I replied.

I knew it wasn't the smartest thing to reply with, but I had no idea what she was going to see. I needed Michelle out of this. Her eyebrows went up, and she tossed my phone on to my bed.

"Fine, but how could you not tell me?" She put her hands on her hips as she gave me one of her looks.

"I don't want to talk about this, please," I said.

"Why are you talking to him? He's a jerk," she demanded.

"I thought you liked him," I said.

"As a person he's fine, but in relationships, he's trash! Absolutely not. Not after he broke my best friend's heart. So you've been seeing him, and you never mentioned this? How could you do that?" she asked accusingly.

"Nothing is happening," I pleaded.

"Right… I'm not going to just sit here and get lied to. If you want to walk on that road of pain again, fine, but don't call me at two in the morning with one of your panic attacks," she said before she ran downstairs.

I felt like the wind had been knocked out of me. I had no words, so I watched instead. I listened as she quickly left the house with a loud slam. I was so frozen, I couldn't even move to wipe the tears rolling down my cheeks. More than anything, I felt like a burden for bothering her with my problems. I wondered if she had always felt that way.

I thought about texting Noah back about the flowers but decided not to. I needed time to think. I needed more answers. I needed something to throw Jason off.

While I tried to figure out how to do that, I looked up the name Eliza Craig online. It wasn't the first time I heard that name. I'd seen her mentioned on social media pages that spoke about the expensive clubs and lounges that rich girls would go to in the city.

At first, there were just articles about rich heiresses. She was the daughter of some ridiculously rich guy named Daniel Craig. I searched on a directory website, but none matched her age. I thought I hit a wall until I searched her name again and realized she had a wiki page. I rolled my eyes. *Of course, she was known enough to have a wiki page*, I thought. I guess it made sense. I remembered finding out Noah had a page made about him once the investigation started. He was rich, young, and possibly a criminal. He also was the child of a man who was pretty famous in his time. Everyone wanted to read about Noah Crawford and the secret life everyone thought he was probably living. What was funny was that they were right—he was.

The first line had Eliza's full name Elizabeth Carol Craig. I went back to the directory and searched the name Elizabeth Craig. There were quite a few, but I soon found one that matched the probable age and location of Eliza. I wrinkled my nose at the ten dollars I had to spend on the site to get the full location and then put it in my phone.

I ran downstairs to see Dad laying on the couch while he watched sports highlights on TV. He sat up when he heard my footsteps. He gave me a questioning look.

"Where are you going?" he asked.

"Just out for a little bit," I answered evasively.

"And where is that?" he asked again a lot more sternly.

I rolled my eyes while my back was turned to him as I reached for my coat. I loved him with every fiber in me, but this was one of those times that I missed my apartment and not having to answer to anyone about where I was going.

"I'm just running to Michelle's," I said, throwing on my coat.

"Oh… busy girl. I heard her leave earlier, but I'm sure you two will work it out... I thought we would get some lunch today," he said, disappointed.

"It's only 10. I'll be back by 12:30, the latest," I said with a relaxed smile.

"Alright," he said before disappearing behind the couch again.

According to the directory, Eliza lived nearby in Garden City. I hopped on the highway, and it only took fifteen minutes to get to my destination. I was so bent on finding out more that I didn't even have the chance to be nervous during the drive.

If Jason was impressed with my town, then his jaw would've been on the floor with the houses in this one. They were massive. Every house garnished with large iron gates, large windows, and a driveway with at least one unnecessarily expensive car. I pulled up to a large gate with a fountain behind it. There was a small security booth nearby, and I drove up to it. A middle-aged man with dark skin and a gray beard slid his window open and nodded politely.

"May I help you?" he asked with a deep voice.

"I'm here to see Eliza Craig," I said.

"Name?" he asked.

"Nicole Smith," I answered.

The man furrowed his eyebrows as he looked through a clipboard with a list of which were probably names. He shook his head after a minute. I already knew my name was not there. I felt my stomach drop. *There it was*. I knew it had to come sometime soon. *Focus on your goal Nicole*, I told myself when I started to feel myself get nervous. He looked up at me.

"Your name is not on the list," he said.

"I'm a ... school friend. If you could just ring her up, I'm sure she would let me in," I said.

"Miss Craig is a busy woman, Ms. Smith," the man said.

I handed him a twenty-dollar bill with a confident smile. I had seen Rachel do this once when she wanted to make it into a private gathering. I hoped I could be just as lucky.

"I'm sure she'll have a moment to answer your call," I said.

The man sighed and picked up a shiny, black phone. It was one of those old ones that had a cord connected. He pressed a couple buttons and waited. I could hear Eliza's voice on the other end.

"What's going on, James?" she answered.

"I have someone here to see you… a girl with the name of Nicole Smith," he said as he glanced up at me.

"*I see*… hmm, yeah, let her in," she said, and I could hear the amusement in her voice.

"Alright," the man said before hanging up.

He nodded to me and pressed a button that made one of the gates open. I smiled before I drove through the opening and up toward the house. I parked next to a red sports car that looked triple the price of my four-year-old SUV and walked toward the door. Before I made it to the top step, Eliza opened the door and gave me an amused, yet scary smile.

"How did you find me?" she asked.

"I have internet access," I deadpanned.

"So what are you doing here?" she asked, standing aside to let me in.

"I have questions, and I know you have the answers," I said before looking around.

There was a huge, dim chandelier hanging from the high ceiling. Behind it was a large spiral staircase that led to the second-floor corridor that looked over the first floor. It was a beautiful house that I'm sure felt creepy when it was empty. The large door made a solid boom when Eliza closed it. I turned around to look at her.

"Bigger is not better in this case. This old place is so dreary most of the time," she said as if she knew what I was thinking.

"I can imagine," I said, completely lying. There was no way I could imagine living here or getting tired of it at that.

"So what are your questions? I might answer them," she said, nodding her head toward the kitchen and I followed.

It was all white with silver appliances. Eliza walked over to the island with her white crop top and light gray sweats and climbed back up to the stool. She started eating a salad that looked like it had chicken and colorful peppers.

"You want one?" she said with her mouth half full.

"A salad? No thanks. I'm fine," I said to the odd offer.

She shrugged and took a few more bites. Then she looked up at me again.

"Questions," she said.

"What can you tell me about The Table?" I asked.

Her eyebrows went up and a smirk formed on her lips. She gave me a once over as if she was impressed. I kept my straight expression. I didn't want to entertain whatever was going on in her head.

"Where'd you hear about that?" she asked.

"I asked you something first," I said.

She rolled her eyes and leaned back to look down a hallway and leaned forward to look down another one. Then she crossed her arms.

"Why didn't you ask Noah? I'm sure he would give you *whatever* you asked for including information like that," she said.

"So you don't have information on it," I said.

"Fine… do you know what the mob is?"

"Um… yeah. Like Al Capone?"

"Eh, kind of. The Table is essentially a network that Noah's dad and my dad set up when they got out of college. Think of a society that makes sure that those who are part of it stay powerful and rich," she said.

I was stunned that she actually answered the question. On the way there, I had practiced how to trick her into telling me. I hadn't planned for this to be so easy.

"Why are you just telling me this?" I asked, unable to mask my confusion.

"Hmm… multiple reasons. One, if you don't figure this shit out with Jason, you'll probably die anyway, and if you do, you'll probably end up part of it," she said.

I stopped and gave her an incredulous look. She chuckled and flipped her auburn hair over her shoulder. I put my hands up and shook my head. There was absolutely no way in hell I would want to be associated with something like The Table in any way, shape, or form.

"I do not want to be part of some secret society that stalks, kills, injures people, and commits crimes," I said.

Eliza rolled her eyes and shook her head at me knowingly. Why did she look at me as if she already knew everything that was about to happen? I didn't like it. Whatever she thought she knew from Noah was only a small part of what there was to know about me. Usually, I would've let myself show my disgust in a situation like this. I didn't let my face move.

"You're already halfway there, honestly. You're the reason Noah isn't in jail. All signs pointed to him. You threw the authorities off and they ran out of leads. You saved him, but simultaneously saved The Table too," she said.

"I did that to protect Noah. It killed me inside doing something like that. You think I did that for personal gain? You're sick," I said.

"No, I don't, but you showed you were worthy. Noah hiding the body after Reggie put him on track for being head," she said.

"Wouldn't killing Reggie be more of a sign?" I asked, pressing my luck on the questions.

"He didn't kill Reggie. You really think Noah Carter Crawford would kill his uncle? No. He's too much of a *pansy*, as his mother would call it, for that." Eliza gave me an incredulous look.

"Then who did?" I asked, deciding I would have to dissect Tracey's comment later.

"Oh… I can't tell you that. I'm not even supposed to know," she said, and for a moment she showed a nervous expression.

"Fine," I sighed.

"My Dad is going to be home soon, so you should go, but before that, I do think you should know that if you do end up with Noah, this is the world you will be part of. My Mom did not want to be part of it either, but she loves my dad so she's here." She shrugged.

"I'm not going to end up with Noah. I moved on," I said.

"Okay, and I think an orange top goes with a purple bottom. Jason is playing you to get information on this case. At least Noah sacrifices his peace every day to make sure you're safe. I hate admitting this, but he's actually in love with you. He's not sure about a lot of things, but wanting you is not one of them." She gave a bitter laugh.

"Noah finds me annoying. You should see how much of an asshole he's been to me," I said.

"He does that so you can listen to him. Duh! He said you were stubborn," she said.

"I should go. Thanks," I said, turning toward the door.

"Wait. I have a question," she said.

"What," I said, spinning around.

"Where did you hear about The Table from?" she asked.

"Jason questioned the Strouses, and it was mentioned by accident... Please don't have one of your minions kill them," I said.

"I don't like the whole killing thing. It's not my thing. It's very... old generation. Plus, Zachary is already crippled, as you know, from his wife's big mouth. I think he knows not to say too much, but you already knew that," she said.

"Right," I said before turning back around to walk away.

I stopped in my tracks and turned around again to look at her. She gave me an annoyed look before rolling her eyes. They bugged his computer. I didn't even need an answer to know that. The only reason I knew that was from Jason. I decided to entertain Eliza and ask.

"How do you have access to Jason's notes?" I asked.

"It's not very hard to get into one's computer these days," she said.

"Speaking of more illegal stuff, who was following me around?" I asked.

"What's the word you used? One of our *minions*," she said mockingly.

I rolled my eyes and left. Eliza shouted "bye" before I walked through the door. I got in the car and sighed. I was overwhelmed by all this information. I was going to start jotting things into a note on my phone, but just in case my phone was being bugged, I wrote a few notes on a piece of paper from my glove compartment.

Chapter 20

I made it home by eleven-thirty. Dad was fast asleep on the couch, so I ran upstairs quietly. I started jotting down things in a little journal I never used. After I transferred my notes from my scrap paper to the journal, I made a to-do list.

1. Find out everything before Jason and skew the information to throw him off.

2. Talk to Noah about everything.

I looked at the list to see if I needed to add anything else when I heard one knock and then the door open. It made me jump. Rachel came through the door with a beige form-fitting turtleneck and dark brown cargo pants with a sash to synch it around her waist. She looked really elegant especially in comparison to my yoga outfit. College had made me not care about outfits as much anymore.

"What are you doing here so early?" I said looking at the time on my clock.

"It's lunch right now and then I had all free periods after calculus, but then Mr. Wise called out sick, so here I am gracing you with my presence," she said as she leaned on my door frame.

"You want to get lunch with us," I said.

"That was the plan," she said, stretching her neck to read over my shoulder.

I closed the journal and spun my desk chair around to face her. She had a mischievous look on her face.

"What's in the book?" she asked.

"Notes," I said.

"What kind of notes?" she asked.

"Notes on this whole situation," I said.

"Can I see?"

"It's probably best if you don't."

"But you said I could help. I have to get briefed on the newest leads."

"Just know Noah's family is part of a secret society and finding out more about it might give us the answers we need," I said as I got up and opened my closet.

"Like the mob? That's kind of badass," she said.

"Shh… and kind of," I whispered.

"They probably have some type of documentation somewhere… There are free tech classes CCT has on Tuesday and Wednesday afternoons for high school and college students. It's part of their give back to the community type programs," she said in an unconvinced voice.

"So?" I asked, grabbing a corduroy skirt and black top from the closet.

"That's cute. We can get into the CCT building and then you can snoop around," she said, throwing me a pair of leggings from my drawer. It was cold.

"I don't know… That could be dangerous," I said.

"Not doing anything is probably worse at this point," she said, matter-of-fact.

She had a point. The idea was probably illegal in some way which would mean that I was committing a crime to hopefully somehow cover up that I committed a crime. It was a risk, and that meant that the sirens started to go off in my head. Then I thought about what Eliza said would happen if I didn't figure things out. For once, I knew I would have to ignore them.

"How do you sign up?" I asked.

Dad brought Rachel and me to an old fifties-style diner. It was one of our favorites. There was classic rock and roll playing when we walked in and waitresses rollerblading on the white and black checkered floors. One of them rolled up to us and then shimmied to the side to stop. She gave us a smile from what seemed to be recognition.

"Hey, guys! A booth for three? Sit wherever you'd like. I'll bring over some menus in a second," she said, running over to a man with his finger up at a booth.

We sat down, and in a couple minutes, we had menus. I already knew what I wanted, but I looked at the menu anyway. Rachel asked if we could share a slice of apple pie, and I nodded conspiratorially. I almost inhaled my burger with fries along with my milkshake. I had a busy morning and realized I never ate a thing. Rachel and I were enjoying our time with Dad, but we both knew what was at the back of our minds—getting to the tech class at 4pm.

"What do you ladies want to do now?" Dad asked after he polished off his plate.

Rachel and I looked at each other. It was two-thirty, and we knew if we didn't head back home in the next forty-five minutes, we would not make it to the course on time. I couldn't think of an excuse, but a smile formed on Rachel's lips. She turned to Dad with a small pout—the one he couldn't resist from his "princess".

"Dad, we would love to do something else, but I have a project coming up and Nicole said she would go with me to the library to help," Rachel said.

"Aw, those are my girls! You have to help each other succeed. I love it." Dad smiled proudly.

He looked so proud, and it made me feel extremely guilty for lying to him. I know Rachel was used to doing it when it came to sneaking around to go to parties or going on secret trips, but I was not. I could count on my hand the number of times I had lied to Mom and Dad. Unfortunately, it felt like it had been happening more often these days. I knew sometimes you had to lie to save someone from pain, but that just meant you had to take on the pain yourself.

I drove us to Queens toward the CCT building. Most of the drive was quiet after Rachel and I formulated our plan. I couldn't help but think about what happened that morning with Michelle. Her words kept replaying in my head. I didn't feel as if I was going to tear up anymore, but I started to rethink some of the moments we had together when I was at my lowest. Was I just a burden to her this whole time?

"What's wrong?" Rachel asked, looking up from her phone.

"Nothing," I sighed.

"Coco, I'm tired of this terrible lying," Rachel sighed.

"Michelle and I got into it this morning," I said, too tired to pretend.

"Really? What happened? You two never argue about anything," she said, putting her phone down.

"She thinks I'm lying to her about not dating Noah," I said.

"*Well…*," Rachel said.

I could see her shrugging and making an amused expression in my peripheral vision. I rolled my eyes. I knew what she was going to say before she even said it.

"What?" I asked.

"You two talk a lot. You've broken up, but still act like it's two years ago. I know the circumstances are different and everything, but it's still a little weird. He like… even still climbs through your bedroom window like he used to. He gets you flowers… I don't know. I know more about this, obviously, but even if I only knew what she knew, I would think something is going on too," Rachel said.

I looked over at Rachel with an incredulous look when I got to a red light. She started to laugh. She put her feet up on my dashboard and rolled her eyes.

"I'm just telling you what I see," she said with her face scrunching as she laughed.

"It's not like that," I sighed.

"I know. It's definitely more him than you, but I don't know… when I was younger, I always felt like I knew you and Noah would get married. Mom and Dad said it too one night. You guys were just so madly in love. I made fun of you two all of the time, but it was cool. I still haven't found 'the one' yet, and I'm three years older than you were when you met him," she went on.

"You're still very young. I'm eighteen, and clearly, I haven't found 'the one' yet either," I said.

I pulled into the parking lot and turned the car engine off. I tied a blazer to my waist. I was going to use my actual driver's license to register for the class, but Rachel stopped me. She handed me her fake ID, which had a picture of her with the name of Yvette Anderson. The name was not funny at all, but I thought it was funny that she had a fake ID and I didn't.

"You're in college. It's so much easier to get alcohol without a fake," she said when she saw the amused look on my face.

"You're insane. Okay, let's go," I said as we walked out of the car.

"What's the plan again?" she whispered.

"I'm going to ask to use the bathroom, and you're going to distract the instructor from noticing I'm taking too long," I said, putting a cap on as a disguise.

"How are you not freaking out over this? It's a little unlike you," she said.

"Internally, I'm freaking out. I'm not doing well at all actually, but I honestly have no choice but to fake it," I sighed.

It was true. My heart was going a mile a minute and breathing wasn't going that well either. Despite that, I kept walking toward the door. There was so much life I had to live. There was so much at stake. I couldn't quit.

"We don't have to do this, Coco," Rachel said softly.

"Yes I do," I said.

We walked in and registered for the class on little kiosks. The secretary told us to wait in a glass waiting room. There were a few other people in the room who looked younger than us. Rachel and I sat at opposite sides of the room. Just in case someone recognized her, we didn't want them to immediately realize I was with her. She faced one side of the glass encasement we were in and I faced another. I got a text from Rachel once a group of people walked past the glass walls.

Rachel Smith: That's the same bald guy that was with the Crawfords last night.
Nicole Smith: I see him.
Rachel Smith: I think that's Noah's mom next to him.

I looked up to see the back of a long dark ponytail that was the same color as Noah's hair before the group went around the corner. I gave a small nod to Rachel before a young guy walked through the door and told us to follow him. We followed him onto an elevator. He typed the numbers 7924 on a little keyboard next to the floor buttons. He pressed the tenth-floor button and we started to move. The man he led us into a computer lab with the newest computers and big glass board in the front of the room. It was so high-tech that it looked like one of those movies where evil scientists talk about some new chemical that will cause chaos or whatever.

Rachel sat a row in front of me. We spent the first twenty minutes listening to the lecture on how to code for a website. I raised my hand and asked for where the bathroom was. Kevin, our lecturer told me, and before I left, I saw Rachel sauntering over to him to ask questions. Kevin didn't stand a chance. I walked down the hall and jumped into an elevator with a guy in a suit. He was about to type the numbers in the keypad, but then he caught me looking at him.

"Where are you headed?" he asked in a nice, but cautious tone.

"The bathroom on this floor has a huge line, so I was going to try another floor. I really have to go," I said.

He gave me a suspicious look, and I immediately felt my scalp prickling. I had to think of an excuse and fast. I thought about what Rachel used as an excuse in school to get out of trouble with male teachers.

"You know… it's that time of the month. Don't want any accidents." I rubbed my stomach.

The guy nodded, and he seemed a little uncomfortable with the topic. It was always funny to me how scandalous the topic of periods seemed to middle-aged men when they, in fact, had wives and daughters who had them every month. It was part of life.

"You can try the eleventh floor," he said before he typed in the code "7924" before pressing the button with the eleven and then the forty-eighth, the highest floor, on it. I got off on the next floor and ran straight into the bathroom right off the elevator. The man watched me until the door closed. I tried to catch my breath since I was pretty sure I didn't breathe during the whole encounter. I gave myself a silent pep talk in the mirror and walked out.

I pressed the button for the elevator. It opened and was empty. With a sigh of relief, I pressed the button with the ten on it as a test, and it brought me down without a code. I walked off and pressed the up button. I got on another empty elevator going up and pressed the button with the forty-eight on it. The elevator did not move. I tried again, but this time I typed in the code "7924" before pressing the button with the forty-eight on it. The elevator went up so fast that I could feel my ears pop. The doors opened and I walked out into a hallway with people in suits walking around. I untied the blazer from my waist and threw it on. I took off my hat and stuck it in the waistband of my skirt in the back so it was hidden from view. With my head down, I walked down the hall.

I was making my way to a little sign with room names on it when I heard a familiar voice coming behind the hallway. It sounded like Tracey. I took a chance and walked into a room full of cubicles to hide. I quickly found one that did not seem to be in recent use and walked in. It had a computer and a file cabinet. I quietly pulled on the cabinet, but it was locked. I took a bobby pin from my hair and tried to pick the lock with my right hand while I got to the login window with my left hand. I smiled for a second at the thought of how proud my sister would be to see this. The computer asked for a pin. My heart sank. I had no idea what the pin was. I tried the elevator pin, but it said: "denied".

I heard a click and realized I had successfully picked the lock on the file cabinet. I opened it quietly yet quickly and looked at the file names. None of them seemed to be of any significance. My eye caught a glimpse of a blank file in the middle of the other ones. It was pushed down so it was almost unrecognizable. I opened it and it had a bunch of passwords. I took a quick picture on my phone and then scanned the pages until I tried the one that was named "desktop". It worked. If I didn't have to be quiet, I would have screamed for joy. I felt like such a badass.

I went directly for a file search and typed in Reginald Crawford. There were two search results. The first file was a document stating a deal made between himself and Carter. I didn't know if it was important. I took the USB drive I had stuffed in my bra out and stuck it in the computer. Before it could sync, the computer asked for another password. I inwardly sighed and opened the file of passwords again and found the password for it. I gained access and dragged the file onto my USB. Then I opened the document that had the date of June 28th from a couple years ago on it. I scrolled. It had different coordinates listed in the beginning along with the words "V-24 Stiletto - T. Crawford". Underneath were a bunch of signatures including Noah's. I didn't have enough time to figure out what it meant so I dragged it to my USB.

I was about to sign out, but out of curiosity, I looked up my name. One file came up. I wasn't ready to open it so I dragged it on to my USB for later. I looked up Jason's name and one file came up on him too. I dragged it over to the USB and then logged off. I looked out to see if the coast was clear. It was. I walked briskly out of the room and then down the hall to the elevator. I pressed the button and it took some time for it to come. I heard a quiet ping and knew it was probably on the floor underneath me. I tapped my foot impatiently as I heard Tracey's voice coming closer from around the corner. I pressed the button impatiently and an empty elevator slowly opened its door. At the corner of my eye, I could see Tracey turning the corner as she spoke to the bald guy. I jumped in the elevator.

"Oh, look. There's one. Hold the door please," the man called.

I cursed underneath my breath and pressed the close door button many times. My stomach was in my throat. I could hear their brisk footsteps coming closer and closer. It closed before they fully came into view and I was safe. I pressed the button with the ten on it and I made my way down. I kept my finger on the close door button to keep anyone else dangerous on the higher floors out. I exhaled deeply and tied my blazer around my waist again. I put my hand on my head in disbelief and I got off on the tenth floor. I ran into the computer lab to see Rachel at her seat with Kevin leaning over to show her something on her desktop screen. She glanced over at me with a small smile before looking back at Kevin with a nod. She was so good.

The class finally ended, and Rachel and I made our way toward the doors. I still felt queasy from my adventure upstairs and yet, triumphant. I was just about to pull the handle on the doors when I heard my name being called. It was Noah. I mean, *who else would it be?*

Chapter 21

Noah walked up to us in a tie and button-down with the sleeves rolled up to his strong forearms. His smile was soft but questioning. I grabbed on to Rachel's hand tight for support. *I was done for*, I thought. He would not want me snooping around, but I wanted answers.

"What are you doing here?" Noah asked with his eyes bouncing between Rachel and myself.

"Hi… what are you doing here?" I asked.

"Err… my mom works here. I'm interning, I guess," he said.

"She's here because I needed one of those computer classes," Rachel said.

"I see… why didn't you tell me you'd be here?" he asked, turning to me.

"Because you suck. Let's go, Coco," she said before pulling me out of the building.

We didn't stop sprinting until we got to my car. We hopped in and drove off before we said a word to each other. Rachel asked me for the USB, and I pulled it out of my bra and tossed it to her. She held it up like it was gold. It was worth the same in my eyes.

Rachel and I ran upstairs to her room to put the USB in her laptop. I was paranoid about the idea of Jason's laptop being bugged. I didn't want to risk putting it in mine yet. I knew Rachel was most likely off the radar. We plugged it in and opened the file about Reginald Crawford's deal with Carter Crawford first. Rachel jot down something on her hand and then started searching for something on her phone. I minimized the window and pressed on the second file about Reggie. I started typing the first coordinate from the file on the computer. The first one showed a spot right off an unnamed lake ten miles away. The second set of coordinates was set by a random warehouse in Williamsburg, Brooklyn. The third was set off a highway in the middle of the woods just a few miles from here.

"What do you think these locations mean?" I asked after a few minutes of staring at the screen.

"I don't know, but look at this article," Rachel said, tossing me her phone.

On the screen was an article with the headline "Crawford Crusade". The article was from seven years earlier, just months before Carter suddenly died. It explained how someone from the inside leaked that the two brothers, Carter and Reginald, were not on good terms due to a disagreement in business management practices. The article also speculated that if there were ever a split between the brothers that Reginald would face more financial losses than Carter, who was the face of CCT Network, as opposed to Reginald, who was only a shareholder. There was a note that the article was taken down.

"Now I may be taking a wild guess here, but I think Reggie might have had something to do with Carter's death," Rachel said.

I was silent because I had already thought about that and was wondering if this would've given Noah reason to kill Reginald. If Noah found out that Reggie did do something, then he could've lost it. The idea of him doing that hurt, but it wasn't because I was disappointed. I had already worked through my disappointment. I felt pain because I wondered if the pain of whatever he knew felt as bad as what I had been trying to let go of for years. Would it cause him to do something the old Noah would never do? Then I remembered that Eliza was so sure that he didn't. She did know more about whoever Noah was recently, but what if she was lying since she was involved in this whole thing herself? What was the truth?

We scrolled past the coordinates and saw the part that said "V-42 Stiletto- T. Crawford". *What did a shoe have to do with this*, I thought. Tracey always wore high heels and the sound of them clicking against the floor right before we could even see her haunted my dreams.

"I don't get why they're mentioning a shoe," I said, pointing to the screen.

"That's not a shoe… that's a type of knife… or dagger rather," Rachel said with raised eyebrows.

"A dagger," I said, taking a moment to process.

"Yes, as in stabbing people," Rachel said.

"Thanks for clearing that part up," I deadpanned.

I didn't have time to wonder why my sister knew what a V-24 Stiletto was, so I continued scrolling through the document and again saw signatures from multiple people, including Tracey and Noah. Did he lie to me? Was Eliza lying? Even if they both were telling the truth, then he was still involved more than he led on. I started to rub my temples.

"Did he… Noah ever seem dangerous?" Rachel asked, probably connecting the same dots I was.

"No… never. He was so kind," I said as my mind went back.

***

I watched the movement of the lake through my tears. I wiped the tears away as soon as they left my eyes, but I was starting to lose the battle.

"Hey, Nicole. Are you okay," a familiar voice asked from behind me.

I turned to see Noah Crawford, the new guy in town, standing behind me with his hands in his pockets. There was a soccer ball at his feet.

"I'm fine," I said, turning back around.

"Oh.. okay. Can I sit with you then?" he asked, but didn't wait for a response before he started sitting down.

"Sure, I guess," I said, tilting my head away from him so he couldn't see my puffy eyes.

We sat there in silence for a while. It wasn't an uncomfortable type of silence, but a silence that you have with someone you know. The thing was, I didn't really know Noah. At least, not that well. Noah had moved into town a few minutes away from my house just a year earlier. He was always tall, but the story was he got all the muscle at some sports camp the summer before freshman year. The girls, younger and older than us, would always pine for his attention. I didn't attempt nor did I need to. Noah and I rode our bikes together on the weekends since the weather had gotten warmer. We always spoke about the most random and weird things. We were becoming good friends.

"You know, I think we already established that I don't do normal stuff all the time, but I don't usually cry when I'm doing fine," he said, looking over at me.

I just shrugged and kept looking forward. Noah didn't say anything but just nodded.

"That's a nice dress. Are you doing something special today?" he asked, trying to start a conversation again.

"Thanks… I wore it for my birthday," I said.

"Oh! Happy birthday! You're fifteen now, right?"

"Yeah… Thanks."

"Welcome to the club. Are you doing anything special for the day?"

"No. I guess not."

"Why?"

"Everyone forgot. None of my friends or family have said a thing."

Noah nodded and then looked back at the lake. I looked over to see him deep in thought. I couldn't understand what there was to think about. I was upset, but I knew I would get over it.

"Well, it's only three in the afternoon. We can still do stuff," Noah said, standing up.

"Like what?" I asked after I took his outstretched hand.

"You'll see," he said with a mischievous smile.

We ran to his house and got his bicycle. I sat on the handlebar, and we were off to an unknown location. I was still upset, but I was also amused by the determination in his eyes. He really wanted me to have a great time and the thought made me smile. Our first stop was the country club at the edge of town.

"What are we doing here?" I asked, hopping off the handlebar.

"Have you ever played mini golf?" he asked as I followed him into a small cabin-like building filled with golf balls and putters.

"No… The only sport I know is cheerleading." I shrugged, embarrassed by what I just said.

"Well it's your lucky day." He chuckled.

I was pretty sure I was about to lose. I wouldn't have been surprised if he was good at this sport too. It was annoying how he was good at every sport. After he clearly lost on purpose and knocked my ball in multiple times, I won by a landslide. He pretended to be devastated by his loss, but I knew it was to make me laugh. It worked.

On our way back to our neighborhood, we stopped at a cool looking thrift store I pointed out. I told Noah we didn't have to go in, but he simply replied with "it's your day". Inside were a bunch of retro clothes. We played around with some of them, and I convinced him to let us take a few embarrassing selfies. Then I noticed it. There was a shiny bar bracelet that had the name Nicole on the silver plate. It was sitting in a pile of other pieces of costume jewelry. I fell in love with it the moment I saw it. Noah walked up behind me when he saw me staring at it.

"Whatcha looking at," he said.

"Just that bracelet. It has my name on it... literally." I chuckled.

"Ooo that is nice…" Noah smiled with approval as he reached into the pile and picked it up.

He helped me try it on and it fit perfectly. I admired it on my wrist for a moment before putting it back. I left the house without my wallet.

"What's wrong? You should get it," he said.

"I left my wallet at home. It's ok." I shrugged.

Noah frowned and picked the bracelet up. He started to walk toward the cashier. I pulled his other arm to stop him.

"No, stop. You don't have to get it for me," I said.

"Okay then I'll get it for me," he teased.

"You're going to wear it?" I asked.

"No. Little bracelets *don't really* go with my style. Let me get it for you." He smiled.

"I don't want you to spend your money on me. That's not fair," I said.

"It's just money. If it'll make you happy, it's worth the forty-five dollars. I want you to be happy... on your birthday especially," he said softly as he reached for his wallet in his back pocket.

I stopped and just looked at him. He didn't realize how sweet his words were. I didn't know how to respond. I found myself looking down at the ground, trying to find the words.

"What a sweet boyfriend. He's a keeper," the old lady at the register winked at me.

"Oh... he's not... we're not dating," I said.

Noah didn't say a thing, but instead, just smirked. His cheeks did get a little red though. He bought the bracelet and then helped me put it on. I wore it out of the store with a sheepish smile on my face.

We walked instead of rode back to my house. It was just five blocks away and the handlebar of his bike wasn't the most comfortable. It gave us some time to talk.

"Do you ever wonder what your birthday will be like fifty years from now?" I asked.

"Hmm... Not my birthday specifically, but just what life will be like. How do you imagine yourself then?" he asked.

"Old. Hopefully, I found someone and had kids with them so then I'll have grandchildren. Then I could be one of those grandmothers who keep a big garden and read stories to her grandchildren. If not, then I guess I'll just travel the world alone," I said.

"You won't be alone." He chuckled.

"How do you know?"

"You're great. Dude, you're so nice to everyone and you do so much."

"There's no need to be crappy to people. Life already does that on its own. And yeah, I like doing things I guess."

"Yeah, but it's more than that. Like my first day at school here, there was a girl alone in the hallway and you spoke to her until she stopped crying. You didn't even know her, but you took the time to make sure she was alright. You probably made her day. Then you are involved in everything. You're in the yearbook club, you volunteer with so many orgs, and you're a cheerleader," he continued.

"Thanks... I just like doing that stuff. It's no big deal," I said sheepishly.

"I know, but just... I remember finding out you do all that stuff, in addition to being nice to me when I first got here. I thought it was really cool. You're really cool. You always have interesting things to say... You're like a movie," he said.

"A movie?"

"Yeah. I thought, she's like a movie. You see her and you're immediately inspired to do amazing things with your life," he said softly.

I chuckled before I wrapped my arms around him and hugged him. I didn't really think before I did it, but I didn't regret it. Noah didn't hug me back. I started to immediately regret the gesture, but then I realized he was holding his bike upright. His mouth curled up into a little smile.

"Thank you… for everything," I said shyly.

"You're welcome… it looks like we're here," he said as we stopped in front of my house.

"I had a great time today," I said as I slowly backed up to my house.

"I aim to please," he said with a smile that was brighter than the sun above us. It would be the first time of many that I would feel my heart skip a beat because of Noah Crawford.

He waved, and I turned around and opened my door. The lights were all off and the house was silent. I flipped the light switch and closed the door behind me. Then a bunch of people rushed out from behind the furniture and screamed "surprise". My mouth dropped open.

"What," was all that could leave my lips and everyone laughed.

"I told you we could surprise her!" Rachel clapped before jumping on me for a hug.

Music started to play and everyone started to crowd around me. I was overcome by emotions and tears started to form at the corners of my eyes. I didn't like surprises, but I appreciated this one.

"Where were you? We expected you to come back like an hour ago?" Michelle asked, placing a tiara on my head.

"I was with… hold on," I said before opening the door and running outside.

I ran out the gate, ran down the block, and turned the corner. I finally caught up with Noah, who was thankfully still walking with his bike and not riding it. He looked confused to see me, but still had a calm and welcoming smile on his face.

"Hello again," he said, and I could see the curiosity in his eyes.

"You need to come with me," I said, pulling his arm with all of my weight.

"Why," he said, turning around his bike without a fight.

"They threw me a surprise party and I want you to come," I said, pulling his arm along.

"You sure? I don't want to impose. I don't know anyone that well yet," he said, matching my quick pace of walking.

"Of course, I'm sure, and you'll get to know them now," I said before dropping his bike on the lawn and pulling him toward the door.

We walked inside, and Rachel stopped us at the door. She looked at Noah with wide eyes and then smiled at me. I tried to tell her to behave, silently with my expression.

"She brought a cute boy." She smiled.

"Rachel," I scolded her.

"No, it's fine. I don't mind being called a cute boy," Noah leaned in and whispered, making me laugh.

It turned out to be one of the best birthdays ever.

***

Chapter 22

After putting off looking at them for the rest of the day, I finally got up and decided to look at the rest of the files the next morning. I didn't want to be disappointed, but I told myself that the possibility of that happening was inevitable. There was nothing great about this whole situation, and something told me that would only become more true the further I read on.

Rachel used her tech-savvy skills and checked my computer for bugs before she removed any tracking data on the files. She transferred all the files over to my computer before she went to school that morning.

After I made myself some tea, I looked at Jason's file first, which was over a hundred pages long. It had information on the surveillance being done on him. It was scary how much information they had. They even had information on his parents, and there was a mention of an older brother I never knew he had. They knew what information he had gathered from the investigation too. He was listed as a high-level threat. I wondered what they did to those they considered threats and why they hadn't done it yet, but quickly pushed the potentially disturbing possibilities out of mind.

I clicked on my name with hesitation. There were endless amounts of information on me too, but I expected that since Noah would know a lot of what was there. What was shocking was that I was listed as an alliance. It read that I had been granted immunity by Noah three years ago. I wasn't sure what that meant. What made him do that before anything was even wrong unless there was already something wrong? Why didn't he change it considering the fact that we didn't speak for two years? How could I have been granted something that I was pretty sure had been a big deal without being told?

The doorbell rang, and my eyes shifted to the time at the top of my screen. It was only 4:30pm, but it was already dark out and I was pretty sure Mom and Dad didn't mention any packages coming in the mail or people coming over. I heard Rachel, who had come home a couple hours before, say she was going to get it so I stayed where I was until she burst through my bedroom door a minute later.

"Jason is here," Rachel said with wide eyes and panic in her voice.

"Uh… where is he," I whispered loudly.

"In the living room," she said before running back downstairs.

I closed my laptop and walked down the stairs. Jason was standing in the living room with an expression that was frightening. It reminded me of the look on his face when he had gotten into that fight with Noah. I finally pulled my eyes off of him and looked at Rachel, who looked mortified. They both looked at me when I made it to the last step, and I could feel the knots in my stomach tightening.

I slowly walked into the living room and shot Rachel a questioning look before I looked at Jason with the friendliest expression I could fake. His expression still did not falter. He knew something. I was sure of it.

"What's up," I finally said breaking the silence.

"I came all the way here to apologize because I felt bad about putting you in the middle of things the other day. I had my suspicions about your relationship with Noah, but now I see that you were working with him all along! You even have your fucking little sister in on it," his voice vibrated against the marble fixtures of the room.

I didn't know how to answer. *How did he know?* I turned to Rachel, whose eyes were glossy like she was about to cry. This was bad. I was the one that cried often, but Rachel hardly did.

"What are you talking about?" I asked, more confused on *how* he found out than what he was talking about.

"He looked at my computer screen. I had his file open," Rachel said in a small voice.

"Maybe next time you want to run surveillance on someone, don't leave documents about it out for them to see," Jason mocked her.

I snapped. I didn't care much about how people came off to me. I had developed a thick skin for things such as people who decided not to use their manners. After everything that had happened with Noah, being his girlfriend did not bring some of the best looks when I was downtown. I had to get used to it. What I never tolerated was someone disrespecting my sister. Despite everything, my emotional armor was nowhere near as tough as Rachel's, so if she got upset, I wanted to fight whatever it was that hurt her.

"Don't you ever talk to her like that again. If you have a problem, then you talk to me," I said, pointing at him.

Jason was silent for a moment. It was almost as if he was in shock. No one ever expected me of being anything but sweet and calm, even when it didn't make sense for me to be. He crossed his arms and lowered his head at me. I crossed my arms and stood tall. *Well, tall for me.* Jason was much taller than me by a long shot.

"Look," Jason said, pinching the bridge of his nose.

"No, you look. We are not having a conversation until you apologize to my sister," I said.

Jason looked at me through narrowed eyes before he looked over my shoulder at Rachel, who had her legs pulled up to her chest on the couch. It was like she was trying to hold herself together.

"I'm sorry… but seriously, you have your sister working with you in doing the Crawfords' dirty work?" Jason asked when his eyes fell back on me.

"We are not working with them," I said with the intention of that being truthful.

"Noah is included," he bit back.

I felt movement behind me, but I didn't look back. I continued to glare at Jason. Rachel was suddenly by my side with wet cheeks. She looked so angry that I momentarily considered whether lasers would come out her eyes.

"Look, Jason. Before you try to play the *moral compass* card, how about we talk about the fact that you've been playing my sister to get leads in this case. That is beyond fucked up," she said, getting in his face.

"That's not true," Jason said uneasily.

"Oh really? If you truly cared about her, you would've never brought her into this," Rachel said.

Jason's eyes looked sad for a moment, but it went away with a challenging look.

"I am doing what's right, okay? I'm sorry it's your ex-boyfriend, but if you're going to sit here and help him, then I'm going to have to bring you down too. I have no choice," Jason said before storming out.

Rachel and I stood in silence as we stared at the door. We didn't know what any of that meant, but we knew it would lead us down a path neither one of us were prepared for. I didn't know what to do so I called Noah. He picked up on the second ring.

"Hey. What's up?" he asked.

"I need you to come here… my place. We need help. Things just got really bad," I said.

Rachel put her finger up to stop me. I looked over at her with a questioning look.

"Maybe we should meet somewhere that won't involve Mom and Dad coming home to chaos," Rachel said.

"When do they come home?" I asked.

"Probably in the next hour," Rachel said, looking at her watch.

I thought for a moment and then it hit me. The apartment. School was closed, but people lived there all the time.

"New plan. Meet me at my apartment in the city," I said.

"Are you in danger?" Noah asked.

"Um… not yet," I said.

"That's comforting… I'll hop on a train. I should be there in the next couple hours," Noah said.

"Perfect. I'll be there around then too," I said before hanging up.

I ran upstairs and grabbed my suitcase that I had failed to fully unpack and threw some essentials in before I closed it up. Rachel stood at the doorway with a confused expression.

"What should I be doing?" she asked.

I didn't know what to tell her. She had been so shaken up by Jason that part of me didn't want to bring her into this any farther. The other part knew that I would need her.

"I don't know, Rachel. Maybe I shouldn't bring you deeper into this," I sighed.

"*Oh no*! I'm going to help you figure this out. I decided to be part of this. I'm going to see it to the end," she said.

"Okay… I don't even know what to have you do," I said, rubbing my temples.

"Jason took a peek at the file on him and the Williamsburg page in another file," Rachel said.

"How do you know that?"

"My laptop shows the times that the files were clicked on. If I'm correct on time… I was upstairs speaking to you around 4:31, and that's when it was clicked on. I happened to see it when he was speaking to you downstairs."

I paced as I tried to sort through all the new information that was floating around in my head. Maybe Jason was headed to Williamsburg, but that was not safe. The address of the warehouse had been mentioned twice in other documents. There was a possibility that members of The Table would be there.

"I'll go to Williamsburg," Rachel said as if it was like a walk in the park.

"Um, no you're not," I exclaimed.

"Why not? You're meeting Noah in Manhattan. Someone should keep an eye on Jason." She shrugged.

"It's not safe," I shook my head.

"Then I'll stay in my car. If something seems amiss, I'll just step on it and get out of there," she said.

"No, Rach," I said.

"We don't have a lot of options here. I'm not going to jail over some shit with Noah *and Tracey*. I'm going. I'll be safe," she said and did not wait for me to answer before she left the room.

I popped an aspirin in my mouth on the train to relieve myself of the headache I was dealing with. My sister was scoping out Jason, who was trying to expose all of us involved in this situation. My headache started to ease by time the train was riding through Brooklyn, but the thought of Rachel being alone in Williamsburg made my heart race and stomach knot. I called her.

"Hey listen, you don't have to do this. I rather you didn't," I said.

"We already went over this. I'm fine. Can I call you back? I'm on the phone with Monica. She's telling me about the party she went to last night," she said with the sound of her indicator light on in the background.

"You're insane," I sighed.

"I'll call you when I get there," she said before hanging up.

I got to my building and pressed the button for the elevator. Noah texted me and told me he had already made it ten minutes ago. I tapped my foot impatiently until I heard the door ping. I dragged my unnecessary suitcase toward the door and then dropped the handle when the doors opened.

"You have to be kidding me." Jason rolled his eyes.

I took a step in front of him to make it harder for him to walk past me. He rolled his eyes and exhaled deeply before taking another step trying to pass me. I took a step in front of him again.

"Jason, we need to talk," I said.

"I'm sorry, but I don't talk to... criminals," he said.

"What? Did you just," I began.

"You heard me. Now, if you could excuse me. I have an appointment in Williamsburg," he said, pushing his way past me.

"Jason... do not go to one of those addresses. It's not safe. We should talk about this," I said.

"Nicole, there were multitudes of opportunities to speak about this. It's too late. I'm sorry. You won't get why, but I have to do this... Tell Noah that he might have to celebrate Christmas early with his filthy-rich family. He might just spend the holidays behind bars," Jason said before walking out the front door.

I pressed the elevator button fervently until the doors opened and I ran in. It felt like it was taking forever and I kept pressing the button with a three on it. The doors opened and I slid my suitcase out in front of me. The wheel got caught on the gap between the elevator and the floor. I was already on the ground when I noticed.

"A woman who knows how to make an entrance," Noah said as he grabbed my arm and helped me up.

"Jason is going to that warehouse in Williamsburg," I said, fumbling over to the door with my keys. I didn't even have time to be embarrassed about the fall.

"Wait he's… okay. You're going to have to explain why the hell you know anything about Williamsburg being important," Noah said, dropping my suitcase once we got in the door.

"Okay, but please don't hate me," I said, leaning on my door for support.

Chapter 23

Noah paced back and forth while I sat on the foot of my bed. He looked sick. The thing was, I had no idea how to fix all of this, so I just watched.

"Say something," I squeaked.

"You… you don't want me to say anything right now." Noah waved a finger in my direction while he continued to pace.

"I figured if I found out everything before he did, then maybe I could stop him," I said.

I had told him everything about that week. He looked like a mixture of mad, confused, impressed, and scared. I think I heard every curse underneath his breath.

"There's just one thing I don't know for sure… What exactly happened with Reggie? Did you do it?" I asked.

Noah looked over to me slowly with the saddest eyes. It looked like he was on the verge of tears. He did not answer.

"So you did? I knew Eliza was lying. Why did you tell me you didn't?" I asked.

"I told you I didn't," he said through his teeth.

"Then who? I know everything else. You might as well tell me. We could all be arrested in a matter of minutes for all we know," I said as I realized the reality of the situation.

"Nicole," Noah groaned.

"Noah, if I have immunity in whatever this thing is, you have to trust me." I stood up.

"I'm protecting you," he said, turning away.

"By not telling me? For years, I dealt with the pain that this whole situation brought me. I dealt with it by myself. At least you have your little society. You don't care. You don't underst—"

"You think I don't understand? I am haunted every day by what my family does and that I have no choice but to be part of it. I didn't kill Reggie. No. If you want to know so bad, then fine. Tracey did. My mother. She killed him in front of me after he tried to snoop around for bank information and told me that he poisoned my father—the only person who had allowed me to just be a kid... My mother is the worst human being I know. You would think as a mother she would tell me it's ok and she wanted to protect me. No. She told me to clean it up. She told me to clean up my murdered, mutilated uncle off the floor. She told me that my father would be disgraced if I didn't take his place at The Table, so I discarded it with some old guys who treated it like it was nothing. You want to know what those locations are? That's where he's hidden. He's cut into pieces. It's sick. I still have nightmares," Noah said with tears running from his eyes.

It was so overwhelming to hear, but I had asked for this. Without trying, I felt tears running down my face too.

"And you think I don't care? About you? Nicole, the first thing I did when I was initiated into The Table was grant you immunity. Tracey hated you, and I didn't put it past her to pull something. Half of the board hates me for all the rules I broke to protect you," he continued.

"Noah, listen—"

"No, you listen! I'm sorry I lied to you. I'm sorry that I did not know how to make that day you walked into the house better, but I care about you so much. If I didn't have you lie… someone could've had you killed by now. It was my only option. Jason is a dick. He does not deserve you. I knew that the moment I looked at him, but I did what I could to protect him because you care about him."

I just nodded. Noah kicked my suitcase across the floor and into the door. The sound was so loud that I jumped. It hurt to see how this was hurting him.

"I'm sorry," I said.

Noah took his sleeve and wiped off his tears. I tried to find the words. My mouth moved as I tried to find the right way to say everything.

"Why would you do all of that for me?" I asked.

"Because I love you," he said bitterly as if he didn't really want to.

"But Noah..," I tried to stop him from saying all of this.

"I fell in love with you almost four years ago, and I never stopped. And every day you look at me without your eyes lighting up like they used to… it breaks me." He lowered his head.

"I don't know what to say to all of this… I don't know if there even is a right thing to say," I whispered from all the emotions in my throat.

"You don't have to say something all the time… Just listen," he sighed with his back turned to me.

It was silent. There was still one pressing question that I couldn't go without asking.

"Why did you not speak to me for those two years… what happened?" I asked.

Noah turned around with his eyes looking behind me, out of focus. They were tired. It wasn't like what happens when you don't get enough rest, but instead what happens when you're looking at something for so long and realize that there is no hope. I prayed my eyes never looked like that.

"I had to go away for a while… One of those places to get help. I was pretty bad," he said, looking down as if he was embarrassed.

I wanted to hug him and tell him that just about anyone would need help after what he had gone through, but I knew it wouldn't help. I stayed in place and watched him take a couple breaths before he continued.

"We moved up to Saddle Rock just a few miles from home, and I told myself I would reach out as soon as I was feeling like myself again, but then when I got admitted that September… I didn't have my phone for like six months. Then, when I got out, I felt like it was too late and you wouldn't want to speak to me," he sighed.

"I wish you did, but I understand," I said softly.

"Yeah… but anyway enough of that. We have work to do," he said, rubbing his jaw as he thought.

"Right… So what's exactly over down in Williamsburg?"

I looked at the clock and realized it had been a while since I had checked my phone. I checked my notifications to see if there were any updates from Rachel. There was none from her, but to my surprise, there was a text from Jason. I hesitated as my thumb hovered over the screen. What if he had called the cops and told me just to gloat? I took a deep breath and tapped on the screen.

"What's wrong?" Noah asked from across the room.

"Jason texted me," I said.

"What did he say?" he asked cautiously as he walked over and read over my shoulder.

Jason Westbrook: S

It was odd, especially because he didn't send a text to explain the one letter. *Maybe he texted me by accident*, I thought. Part of me didn't want to text him back, but if he was going to give me a heads up, I would not give up the chance. I texted him back.

Nicole Smith: What's going on?

I waited a while for a response, but there was nothing. I looked up to see Noah texting feverishly on his phone. His face was scrunched as he typed away on the screen.

"It probably was a mistake. He might not be in the mood to speak with you right now," Noah sighed.

"Who are you texting?" I asked, chuckling at his facial expression.

"Eliza," he said, glancing up.

"She's interesting," I said.

Noah rolled his eyes and shook his head. He tapped his screen a few more times before jamming his phone back in his back pocket.

"She's annoying," he said, putting on his jacket.

"She cares about you… I think," I said.

"I'm going to kick her ass for telling you stuff," he said dryly.

"Where are you going? We haven't figured out anything yet," I said.

"I'm going to find Jason. I think I figured out a plan," Noah said.

"You know where he is?" I asked.

"I'm guessing by the address he saw… Williamsburg," he said.

"What's there? You never told me. There aren't open fields to bury… uh… do stuff like that in Brooklyn," I said following him to the door.

"First of all, you're wrong. Brooklyn has lots of space in some parts… not that I have a lot of experience having to find a spot to hide things, but just saying. Anyway, it's an abandoned warehouse from what I know, but I'm going to find him and speak to him," Noah said.

"And say what?" I asked.

"I will tell you after… it's safer right now if you're in the dark. I need to find him before this gets out of hand," he said with an apologetic frown.

"Fine," I said.

Noah turned to leave out the door, but right before he closed the door, he came back into the apartment and pulled me in for a quick hug. It took me by surprise, so I just stood there.

"I would've preferred if you didn't turn into a whole spy and risked your safety the way you did, but that was kind of badass… so I'm proud of you. You don't do the whole danger thing, and I know that took a lot. Good job, Nikki," he said with a small smile.

Before I could say anything he left, and I was all alone.

Chapter 24

I checked my phone once again to see if Jason had called or texted me. He hadn't, but I had three missed calls from Mom. She probably saw the note on the refrigerator Rachel left.

Going to a party in the city with Coco. Staying at her apartment.

I wanted to fight her on it, but we had no time. I knew Mom was going to let me have it on the phone. I took a deep breath and called her back.

"Hey, Mom! Sorry, I didn't see you calling me," I said, trying to sound as nonchalant as possible.

"Nicole… I had no idea you and Rachel were going out tonight," she said with an edge to her voice.

"Yeah. Rachel wanted to come along to a party I got invited to." I tried to laugh to lighten the mood, but the silence from the other end told me she was not having it.

"You brought her to a *college* party? She is *not* in college yet," she finally said.

I could hear the disapproval in her voice. It was a foreign feeling, having it geared toward me. Usually, I would hear it being used towards Rachel, who didn't really care. I did.

"It's no big deal, Mom. It's not a big party. It's… a," I began to look around the apartment for something to give me inspiration.

My eyes fell on my biology textbook on my nightstand. If there was one thing Mom always had a soft spot for was my tendency to go to, what Rachel referred to as, nerdy events, especially ones that involved science. She said she used to do the same. She met Dad when he went into the wrong building and walked into a biology club meeting. He asked her where the black frat party was. *Yes,* there was only one. Anyway, he never made it to the party. They spoke all night, and he started coming to the biology club meetings to see her. Mom had fond memories of her years in the biology club.

"It's an event for the biology majors… We talk about our career goals and mingle, and it's also Christmas so the New York kids are having a party," I said.

Mom was silent for a while. It made my heart beat at a rate I was pretty sure was unhealthy for someone standing still.

"Rachel wanted to go to your bio club's holiday party?" Mom asked with a dry voice.

"Yeah! She wanted to get a feel for what college is like I guess," I said trying to sound as if I too was surprised by my sister's choices.

"Well, alright. Where is she now? Can I speak to her?" she asked.

I mouthed a few curses underneath my breath. I stomped in frustration. How was I going to pull this off? I started to pace around and found myself in the bathroom.

"I'm in the bathroom right now. I'll tell her to call you when I go back out to the party," I said, surprised that I could think of something like that.

"Oh, that's fine. I'll text her then," she said.

"Really? I mean, ok cool," I said in shock.

"Good night. Have fun," she said before hanging up.

If I could give myself a high five then, I would. I couldn't help but think how proud Rachel would be of me for pulling that off. I called her after making a cup of celebratory tea.

"You told Mom we're at a biology party? You're such a fucking grandma. Have you not been paying attention for the past seventeen and a half years of my life? Why the hell would I want to be there? If you weren't totally badass for what you did yesterday at CCT, I would call you lame," Rachel answered the phone.

"Sorry! She seemed pissed you were at a college party. I had to say something that would not make her go in tyrant mode," I said.

"Yeah, yeah, whatever. I just got into Williamsburg. I'm like ten minutes away from the address," she said.

"How was the ride over? Everything went ok?" I asked.

"It was fine, just lots of traffic. Again, I'm dealing with city traffic for you, and this time it's the holidays," she said with a sigh.

"I said you didn't have to do this," I said.

"I told you that you're not leaving me out of this. Anyway, I'll call you back in a few. Kadeem is calling me," she said.

"Who the hell is Kadeem? Can't he wait?" I asked.

"No, he can't. He's high on the list for potential prom dates," she said.

"Rachel! There might not be a prom if you are not ___"

"Careful? Serious about this? I know. Give me a few minutes. Bye!"

I threw my phone on my nightstand and rubbed my temples. *When this is over, I have to have a long talk with her about priorities*, I thought. She kept texting me to wait five more minutes, and five minutes turned into twenty before I decided that taking a moment to rest my eyes was in order. I needed the stress headache that I was plagued with to go away. My mind started to go back to a memory.

***

Noah's eyes were tired when I opened the door to let him in that morning. I was about to ask him what was wrong when he pulled me in for a passionate kiss after closing the door behind him. He pulled away and rested his forehead on mine before he started kissing me again.

"Okay, okay, relax now," Dad called with his head leaning out of the living room.

"Good morning, Mr. Smith," Noah called, still hugging me tight.

I heard Dad sigh before he went back to what he was doing. Noah was not the extra PDA type. Something was wrong.

"What's gotten into you?" I asked.

"I'm just really happy to see you... You're my escape from everything at times," he said before sucking on my lip hard.

I pulled away and put him at arm's length so I could just look at him. He looked down like he was avoiding me, even though he was right here.

"What happened?" I asked softly so my Dad wouldn't hear.

"Things are a lot with Reggie being at the house, and that's in addition to my mother being… her," he said softly back.

I nodded and pecked him on the lips again before I hugged him.

"I know you'd rather not, but if you ever want to vent, I'm here for you," I said, putting my head on his chest.

"That's okay, Nikki. I'm alright," he said, but I could feel how tense he was. I wished he didn't stress as much as he did.

"If I could make it go away, I would," I said.

"And that's more than I could ever wish for… Someone who takes it all away even for just a moment. I love you," he said before kissing my forehead.

"I love you more," I said, looking up at him.

"Let me take you to breakfast," he said, looking down at me with the longest lashes that framed the greenest eyes.

"I just ate an hour ago," I said.

"That means you can eat again." He smirked.

"That means I'll get fat if I keep eating whenever you offer to feed me." I chuckled.

"Fat? You're so small," he said, grabbing my waist.

"I'm decent," I said.

"You're perfect," he whispered, nuzzling my ear.

"Thank you, but I am not." I laughed at the tickle.

"I could show you how perfect I think you are," he said, grabbing my butt and then suddenly letting go of me.

I heard Dad clear his throat, and I turned around to see him standing right there. Noah stood up straight before shaking his hand. I could tell he squeezed Noah's hand extra hard.

"How's everything, Noah?" Dad asked.

"Good. We were just about to go to breakfast," Noah said.

"Really it's him getting breakfast and me picking off his plate because I already ate," I said before grabbing a jacket from the coat closet.

"I see… Have fun, kids," Dad said before raising an eyebrow at Noah that made his shoulders fall a little.

I knew I would hear about it later, but that was better than that moment. I pulled Noah out the door and walked over to his car. It was a Saturday morning, and it was quiet on my block. I looked up at the street and could've sworn I saw Tracey standing in the distance. I looked down to make sure I didn't miss a step, but when I looked back up, no one was there.

"Did you see your Mom just now?" I asked, looking around.

"Um, no. You're probably just thinking about what I said," he said, putting on his sunglasses and turning up the music on his car stereo.

***

Chapter 25

I still had my eyes closed as I drifted out of my dream when I felt like I heard someone in the apartment with me. I tried to stay still as I listened for any movement. There was nothing, but I still felt like I was not alone. I kept my eyes closed as I turned over. I heard footsteps move around toward the window across from the kitchen. I wanted to open my eyes and turn back around to see what it was, but I was too scared of the truth. This was worse than checking my portal for final grades, or even opening college decision letters.

I kept counting to three to will myself to open my eyes, but each time, I found an excuse to not do it. I listened for more sound, but there was nothing else. That was, until my phone started to vibrate against the nightstand. My eyes flew open involuntarily, and I reached for my phone. It was a message from Michelle. I caught a glimpse of something going out of the window before I looked back down at my phone. I got distracted when I saw how long the message was.

Michelle Solomon: Hey. I know I said some really messed up things. I'm sorry. I should've never said that. You're so strong for what you dealt with and I know I will never understand. I know you probably don't want to talk to me right now. I completely understand, but I would love it if we could talk about things when I get back from Trinidad after Christmas.

I smiled at my phone before I slipped it in my pocket. I slowly walked over to the window, but no one was there. I mentally retraced my steps since I entered the apartment. None of them involved me opening a window in the middle of December. I walked over to the window, closed, and locked it. I walked over to my nightstand to get my cup of tea but stopped when I noticed some white powder around it. *That's odd*, I thought. I didn't eat anything that was covered in powdered sugar or something similar. I smelled the cup, it smelled normal. I decided to throw the tea in the sink and saw the sponge start to disintegrate. The melted components started to run down the drain. I backed up from the sink mortified, and my stomach started to feel sick immediately. *What was in my tea?*

I looked at the clock on the wall. It was after ten, and I hadn't heard a thing from Rachel, Noah, or Jason. I grabbed my phone from my back pocket and checked the screen for notifications. There was only one from Rachel with a bunch of question marks as the message. I called her and she answered immediately.

"Hey. Please tell me you're heading back home, and Jason is safe or something," I said.

"No. Shit. Is your door locked?" she asked in a panicked voice.

"Um, yeah. I think so," I said.

"Check!" she almost screamed.

I walked over and turned the knob. The door opened, and my stomach fell. I turned the lock and slid the chain into the lock position. I turned on every light in the apartment and grabbed a kitchen knife.

"Okay… now it's locked. What made you ask?" I said, putting my back against a wall.

"I think I saw someone running out of your window and down the fire escape… I'm not sure, but I'm pretty sure that's your apartment. I almost shat myself when you didn't answer your phone," she said.

"You never called me," I said.

"I called you *seven* times," she said.

I put my phone on speaker and checked it for missed calls. There were none.

"I didn't get any," I said slowly, in fear.

A chill started to creep up my back. The feeling that I didn't have an ounce of control of whatever was happening made my heart race. The thing was, I didn't have time to freak out. I had to take action. The question was how would I do that?

"I need you to go home, Rachel. Are you out of the car?" I asked.

"No, I'm still in the car. What about you? You have to get out of there," she cried.

"I don't know if it is safe for me to leave this apartment, or even be in this apartment, but I'm staying here for now. I need you to go home," I said.

"Nicole, I think Jason might be dead. He went into the warehouse, and then I heard gunshots. I'm not sure what's happening. We have to do something," she said.

"What? How long ago was this?" I asked, looking at the clock that read 10:32.

"Like almost an hour ago! I couldn't get through to you," she said.

"I need you to go. Now. I don't care what's going on," I said.

An intense banging sound began to sound from my front door a moment later. I jumped so high, I'm surprised I didn't hit the ceiling. The chain from the lock began to swing a little. I took a step with my knife toward the door. My heart started to beat so fast this time, that I wondered if it was fear, a heart attack, or both.

"What's that?" Rachel asked.

"Who is it," I called.

The banging continued, and then there was a more intense bang like someone was trying to break in. The room vibrated. I held on to the knife so tightly that my hand started to hurt.

"I said who is it," I said louder.

"It's Noah. What's happening?" the voice yelled back from the other side of the door.

"Where's Jason?" I asked, looking through the peephole.

"I don't know. I turned back around when Rachel called me and told me something was wrong," he called.

"Rachel, you called Noah?" I asked.

"*Yeah*. I still had his number from before. I thought something was wrong. I hate him, but you being alive is more important," she said.

"Please drive. Now," I said.

"Okay, fine. I'm driving," she said, and I heard the car's engine.

I unlocked the door, and Noah walked in. He started to look around and then stopped when he saw the knife in my hand. He narrowed his eyes in confusion.

"What happened?" he asked, locking the door behind him.

"Someone was here," I said.

Noah froze before he got close and put his hands on my shoulders. He examined me before he started to walk around.

"I didn't drink it," I said, and I wanted to cry because I thought about what would've happened if I did.

"What?" he asked after a moment.

"There was white powder thrown into my tea. I threw it out, and my sponge started to melt," I said.

"Holy shit," Rachel screamed in response, and it made us both jump.

"Where are you?" I asked.

"I'm on the FDR... the highway," she said.

Noah slowly walked over to the sink and made a face at the sponge. Then he went back to look at the powder in the shape of a circle where my mug was. The silence of the moment was ear piercing.

"I need to get you out of here," he said.

"What is it?" I asked, immediately frightened by his expression.

"I... I don't entirely know," he said, looking around in what looked like disbelief.

"Someone tried to... poison you?" Rachel asked in a tone that was nothing less than horrified.

"I don't know," I said.

My phone started to chime. I gasped loudly. Noah walked over to me and looked over my shoulder. Jason's name was on the screen.

"Rachel, stay on the line. Jason's calling," I said.

"Okay, good. I'll hold," she sighed in relief.

I switched to the other line and heard weird breathing on the line. Noah and I looked at each other with a look of confusion before looking back at the screen.

"Hello? Jason," I answered.

"This is not Jason," a distorted voice answered.

Acknowledgements

Thank you, God, for all your blessings, especially for giving me the strength to endure this long road of a project.

Thanks also to: my family for always supporting me in all my endeavors and for our fun, everlasting debates about this book and the ones on the way.

My friends, who kept me going while writing this in grad school. Without our conversations and adventures, I would be without inspiration. Like their support over the years, my love for my friends and family is endless.